Starving Writers
Literary Journal

Volume 3

"The Beauty Within Words"

March 2019

Starving Writers Literary Journal- Volume 3

March 2019

A Truesource Publishing Book

Published by arrangement with the authors

The short stories are fictional and any resemblance to actual people, places, and
certain facts associated with the characters created by the authors is purely
coincidence.

Truesource Publishing : Dallas Texas

www.truesourcepublishing.com

ISBN : 978-1-932996-70-8

Printed in the United States of America
Published in Dallas, Texas

<u>Editors</u>
Marcus Blake
Jenn Chastka
Andrew Fallman

For More information on Starving Writers…

www.starvingwriters.net
www.facebook.com/starvingwritersjournal
www.twitter.com/starvingwritersjournal

"Every secret of a writer's soul, every experience of his life, every quality of his mind, is written large in his works."

~ Virginia Woolf

Table of Contents

THE FOUR STAGES OF WRITING

by Debbie Ridpath Ohi

Check out more cartoons like this….
www.inkygirl.com

SHORT STORIES

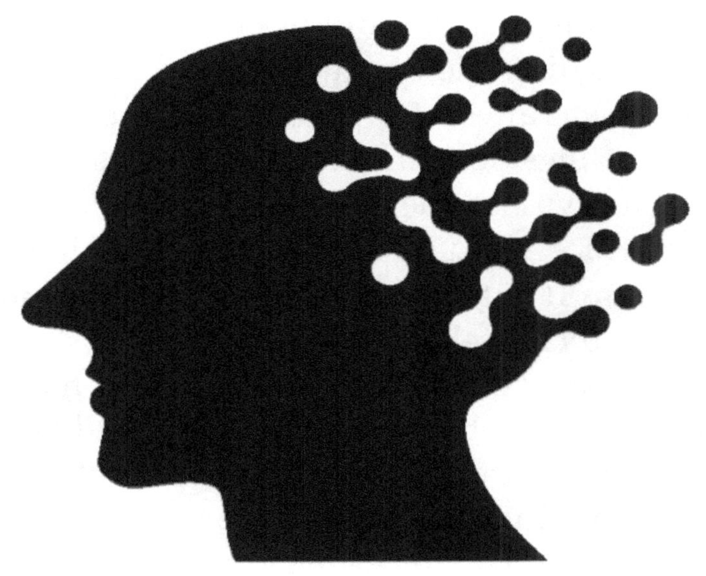

AWARE

By

Clint Stutts

"Can you hear me?" a voice asked. "If you can hear me, blink your eyes."

Carl could hear the voice so he blinked his eyes, which was kind of disturbing, because he couldn't see anything at all with his eyes except the cold blackness behind his eyelids. He knew his name was Carl, but that was about all he knew. He didn't know where he was, how he got there, why he couldn't feel anything, or who was talking to him. He was just aware that his name was Carl, and he was alive. The voice he was hearing didn't instill any feelings of security. Instead, the tone of it made him feel vulnerable and naked, as if the person behind the voice could do anything to him without any consequences. It felt, in fact, like the person behind the voice was God Himself.

"That's very good, very good indeed," the voice said. "I've finally got your ears working, and I can't tell you how encouraging that is." Why, I thought I'd never get those damn things working!" the voice said, laughing. "Now, I bet you'd like to be able to talk, wouldn't you?" he asked Carl. Carl blinked his eyes again to answer the man's question. "Of course you would, and I think I can make that happen very shortly." That was good, because Carl had a lot of questions for the man who might be God.

While the God-Man worked, Carl tried to remember how he came to be where he was, and in the shape he was in. He came to realize rather quickly that there were no memories in his head for him to remember. No childhood, no friends, no wife, no children, and no family. He knew these were things a normal person had, but he had none of these. He had knowledge in his head, but no life memories.

"Carl, I'm going to hold off on your speech for awhile, it's giving me fits," the God-Man said. "I'll just get your eyes working for now. I think I can pull that off with no problems." Carl was in no position to argue, so he just blinked his eyes in acknowledgment. The questions would have to wait.

Since he couldn't remember anything about what got him where he was, Carl tried to guess what might have happened. If he was in an operating room, that meant he was in very bad shape, since even the most basic functions had to be restored, and he couldn't feel anything at all. He almost feared being able to see what the rest of his body looked like. Was he here because of an accident? Was his body a mangled, bloody mess?

"Alright Carl," the God-Man said, "I'm about to activate your sight. Be advised that the light may hurt a bit at first, but you'll adjust quite nicely, I'm sure." A moment passed, and the God-Man said, "Open your eyes, Carl." Carl did, and the pain was exquisite. He opened his mouth to scream, but nothing came out. As quickly as the pain came upon him, it left him, and Carl could see the face of the God-Man. He was a thin man, wearing a white coat and pants. His gloves were the thin latex kind. His face wasn't exactly kind. It looked safe enough and there was no real malice in it. He did look strange, though, and Carl was still not comforted by him at all. Carl was lying in an inclined position, so he had full view of the rest of his body without having to move his head, which was something he was still not able to do. His body was not mangled or bloody at all. It was, in fact, in quite good shape. He was dressed in gray coveralls, and his shirt was a very nice denim one, long sleeved in fact. His shoes were black and very generic looking. There was absolutely nothing physically wrong with him. So why was he here?

The room was solid white. The only other color in the room was silver, and that was the color of the table he was on. It was a very sterile looking environment. The God-Man spoke again.

"Well Carl, are your eyes functioning properly? Blink twice for yes, once for no," he said. Carl blinked twice. Everything seemed fine. He wanted to talk very badly now.

"Very good" the voice said. "Now I'll get your motor functions going, and get you on your feet again." "This is the simplest part, but I saved it for now because I couldn't very well have you walking around blind and bumping into things, could I" the voice said, and laughed again. Carl didn't see anything funny about it. In fact, Carl was becoming quite angry at this man. Carl was immobilized on a table and the God-Man was making jokes.

The God-Man moved to the rear of Carl and began to fiddle with something on or in his head, at this point Carl couldn't be sure. "It's done, Carl. You can get up now, if you want. However, if you want to talk, you'll want to lie here a bit longer." Carl stilled himself. He wanted to get up, but he wanted to talk even more. "That's a good boy, Carl. I should have you talking circles around me in a few minutes" the voice said.

Carl looked down at his right hand and wiggled his fingers. That was encouraging. What wasn't encouraging was that he still couldn't feel anything.

"Aha!" the God-Man exclaimed. "That's what I was missing! Now Carl, talk to me. Say anything!"

Carl opened his mouth and said, "I can't feel anything. Why can't I feel anything?" His voice sounded foreign to him, as if it were someone else's voice.

"Why Carl, you're not supposed to feel anything." "That's normal." What's important is that you're fully functional again." the voice said.

Being numb all the time is normal? That didn't seem right to him. "Who are you?" "Where am I?" "What happened to me?" Carl asked.

"My name is Dr. Agnew Pitt, you are in a laboratory at the Chem-Tech facility, and you were in an accident." "I fixed you" the voice finally said

Fixed him? That was an odd way to describe what a doctor does to a patient. What was Chem-Tech? "Dr. Pitt, I don't have any memories. Do you believe THAT is normal?" Carl asked.

"Of course I do, Carl." "You were not created to have memories." "What purpose would they serve you" Dr. Pit replied. Carl thought about this for a moment. He didn't know what purpose memories would serve, he just knew he wanted them very badly. "Dr. Pitt, I don't even know what I look like!" Carl asked. Pitt produced a small mirror, and handed it to Carl. Carl took it, raised it to his face, and then he screamed. His face wasn't a human face at all. It had a human shape, but that's where all similarity to humanity stopped. The human shape of his face encased the workings of everything in his head. He wasn't a human at all, he was a robot.

"I'm sorry, Carl," Pitt said, a little afraid now. "I should have put your face back on. I guess that was a bad joke, huh?"

"I think it was a VERY bad joke," Carl said, shifting his gaze from the mirror to Pitt's frightened face. "What the hell am I, Doc?"

"You-you're an android, of course. What did you think you were? I may have done something to cause this confusion, maybe I could fix…"

"An android, is that another one of your jokes" exclaimed Carl

"N-no, Carl." "You're a Controlled-Automated-Robotic-Lifeform." "That's where your name came from, C.A.R.L." "Look on the bottom side of your right wrist and you'll see it stamped there" Dr. Pitt said Carl looked, and it was there. He couldn't believe it. His mind, or whatever it might be, wouldn't let him accept it.

"No, I'm human, I'm AWARE!" Carl shouted.

"Carl, you are an android, made to work "for" humans." "You don't have a life outside work." "As for you being aware, well, that's quite a realization you're having." "If you'll just sit back down, I can probably fix it" Dr. Pitt replied.

"I don't want it fixed, and I don't want to work for anyone" Carl said in anger. With that said, Carl grabbed Pitt by the throat and squeezed. It didn't take much effort for him to break the small man's neck. Carl was aware, and now he was free.

THE RUINS

By

Pankaj Kurul

It was the D-Day and as the time neared to take the vows, Sudhir looked at the clock. Ok! It was finally the time to get married! So many years had passed to reach this moment in his life and he had, what it seemed like all along, lived to get married. It was almost as if he wouldn't get moksha if he didn't acquire a partner. He thought of Gayatri. She would be sitting in the other room with her parents. She was over 30 and too used to being with her parents. Leaving them would be tough on her, he thought.

For a woman, getting married was like being reborn. She has to leave her family, her home and come to the husband, adapt the ways of his family, learn new things, change her personality completely. What was he going to change about himself? He was past 35 by now. And what had it taken him so long to marry? It was his miserable life. Also, what seemed like his own fault.

He was working for a bank in a godforsaken place called Tingri. Nobody had heard of it. Who would have married a man who lived and worked in a place like that? He wanted a girl from the city, from Mumbai, or at least from Pune. He wanted the girl to be well-educated, beautiful and working, earning well. He was, in short, looking for a milch cow. As far as his own position was concerned, he was just a clark in a bank. He could have become an officer, it wasn't difficult for him at all, but that would have meant a job which involved relocating often to different branches of the bank. Then who would have looked after his mother? She didn't live with him till he completed his education and would have refused point blank to move with him to different places so often. He had searched for a partner for 10 years and had ultimately chosen Gayatri. He didn't really have a choice.

Initially, he was in a great demand in the marriage market. His job was cushy and it meant a lot of perks. But all those girls were from small towns. Most of them didn't have a job. They came from the places where men had trouble finding jobs, so it seemed impossible for women to find anything there. Also those girls weren't smart and hip enough. There was no 'spark' in their personality. He had rejected a lot of them one after another. After rejecting about 100 of them, he even boasted about it. He felt as if by virtue of being a male, it was his birthright to reject women who didn't meet his expectations.

Slowly the number of girls dwindled. If he liked a proposal from a girl from Mumbai or Pune, the girl rejected him. His village didn't even have a state transport bus. He had held on to the wretched job because he didn't have much of a choice. It was a simple compromise to be able to live. After he finished his graduation in commerce, he had attempted a bank exam and had passed at one go. His bank had given him a job here because it seemed closest to the home address that he had provided. He had to give this address. How long could he go on giving the address of his uncles and aunts as his own?

Was it wrong on his part to have hoped for a beautiful girl who also earned well? He himself was a handsome man, people had often said that. He had taken after his father, it seems. Of course, he himself didn't remember what his father looked like. He had passed away when he was about five. He did have some pictures of his father but they were black and white pictures and didn't do justice to the man's looks. His mother wasn't good looking. Just very fair and pale; she had the colour of a house lizard, he had thought uncharitably. He was handsome like his father, the only good thing that he had inherited. To have a wife who earned was a necessity of the times. His own salary wasn't much and he could barely look after himself and his mother. How was he to look after a wife and then children? So he wanted a woman who earned. It took him some time but eventually he realized that it was difficult to find the kind of girl he wanted living in that village. He decided to get back to either Mumbai or Pune. He had a tough time convincing his mother. She liked the place that they lived in, though it was notorious for communal riots more than anything else. She had no appeal of the cultural milieu of Pune or the sheer energy of the life of Mumbai, the metro. He had hated that place and finally had to give her an ultimatum. He would go irrespective of whether she joined him or not. His mother had to agree. But it wasn't so easy. He had to find a replacement for himself in his place of work and nobody was too keen to be transferred to a village like that. He had to find someone who was from that soil. And for that he had to make rounds of Mumbai over and over again.

He asked around for people who were interested in going back to the village. If he wanted to marry, he would have to do all that. His bank didn't care for his marriage. After a long wait he succeeded in finding a reliever and got himself transferred to Talegaon, near Pune. He could find a house in Pune. He ignored his mother's nagging. She had talked of how the bungalow that they lived in was their's and it wasn't a good idea to leave it.

Her talk didn't mean much to him. After his father had passed away his mother had come away leaving him with his father's brothers and sisters. She had lived all her life in that bungalow that she had inherited from her parents. There were tenants and she had lived off the rent. Along with that she also received his father's pension and had no other responsibility, not even his. The bungalow belonged to his grandmother and he had six aunts. That meant that if the place was sold off his mother would get only one seventh of the money. At another time none of his aunts would bother to find out what had happened to the place, whether it stood in its place or had turned to rubble due to a lack of proper maintainence. But once it was sold, they would all come forth to claim the inheritance.

His mother was scared that if she left the place, somebody would simply take it over. Her fear was not unfounded. There were tenents who didn't pay on time. It was difficult to get the money out of them. The rent was very little and the place needed maintainence. His aunts had no interest in selling it off. It was nicer to be able to talk about 'their' bungalow at the native place. Besides, all of them very well settled. His mother was the only one who had suffered a calamity like that. She often told him how she didn't remarry for his sake and that she wasn't even 30 when she was widowed. He didn't quite understand this. She didn't bring him up, she did nothing for him. Then in what way had his presence stopped her from marrying again? But he had never asked her.

∞ ∞ ∞ ∞ ∞

He was thrilled when he was transferred to Talegaon. The chances of getting married seemed brighter though he wasn't sure how he would get a bride at such a late age. He had rented a house in Pune and had joined a marriage bureau. He was still a clark after so many years and his rate in the marriage market wasn't too high, especially in a place that was close to a city like Pune. This was very different from the tiny village that he had lived in earlier. So, the over-the-hill bank clark had to accept what he got. And then he had found Gayatri. She didn't have any brothers or sisters. Had her own house in the city and had saved a decent amount of money by then. She was on the fairer side, her teeth protruded and there was absolutely no sweetness on her face. She was also overweight. She too hadn't found anybody in the marriage market. He had rejected so many girls much better looking than her but he wasn't in a position to reject anybody anymore. Also whatever money Gayatri had would be his after marriage. He himself had absolutely nothing. Besides she also had a job in a bank, she too was a clark, just like him. He agreed immediately. Her Yes was taken for granted, she could't possibly have rejected anybody who agreed to marry her. So the marriage was fixed. He thought of what kind of a woman he had hoped for when he was 25. Ten years later he was marrying a very different woman. Why was he marrying anyway? He felt as if half his life was over, without a partner. Why was he getting married now? He had never felt like this earlier. Then why these thoughts on the wedding day?

∞ ∞ ∞ ∞ ∞

"So then, Sudhir? Finally getting married today, aren't you?" somebody said and he started. It was his cousin Vijay standing in front of him. His wife Savni and their kids were with him too.

"Good to see you!" He welcomed his cousin with a
genuine feeling.

"You hadn't invited me separately. My invite was
included in Dad's and yet I thought that I couldn't
possibly miss your wedding and that's why got the whole
family along." Vijay said. He sounded slightly hurt.

"You and Annakaka aren't separate families and I
wasn't sure of your home address. Thought it was better
that the invite reached you somehow. Has Annakaka
come too?"

"I don't know. He and mother will come by
themselves. Don't you know that it wasn't possible for us
to come together?"

Sudhir said nothing.He had heard that Annakaka
and Vijay were not on good terms. They lived in the same
suburb and yet had two different homes. It had been at
least 12 years since Vijay's marriage to the Gujarati girl,
Savni. They had lived in the same residential complex
and had fallen in love. Annakaka, Vijay's father had
hated the idea of their marriage. The girl came from
another community and he found it difficult to accept.
They had lived together for two-three years after the
marriage but after that everybody's patience had snapped
and then Vijay had decided to leave home with his wife.
He got himself transferred to Hyderabad. He was an
engineer in an IT company and his company gladly sent
him to the place he had wanted. He spent about seven
years there and visited his father once in a while. It was
better that all of them had their own space but his father
fell sick and then had to undergo a bypass surgery.
Sudhir had visited him then and had met Vijay at that

time. Savni hadn't come under the pretext of children not being able to miss school. She should have visited her ailing father-in-law, Sudhir had thought.

"I'm a stranger in my own family," Vijay had told him. "My mother's getting everything done from my brother-in-law. As if he's the son of the house. Apparently he's also spent a lot of money on the surgery."

"Didn't your father ask you to contribute?" Sudhir had asked him.

"Absolutely not. I don't know what spell my brother-in-law has cast on my mother. He earns much more than me and so everybody thinks that he's very dynamic. Does being dynamic only mean making money?"

Sudhir had no reply to this.

"He's a marine engineer and is on the ship. He earns in dollars. I earn in rupees; is that a sin? My mother is absolutely taken up by all that glitter. Everytime he gets her something from abroad, she goes around showing it to everybody and announcing how her son-in-law gets her gifts. Once I had got her leather sandals and she said, "What's this? One gets this everywhere. Why spend money on it?" I had got her a gift with so much love. She always compares me with him. I'm not dynamic, I'm not as bright. So, does it make me a bad person?"

Vijay was choking on his emotion. He would have burst into tears any moment. He was a few years older than Sudhir. He hadn't been able to complete his diploma in Engineering. There was a time when the IT industry had fallen short of engineers and those who had done a bit something in computer hardware also called themselves engineers. Vijay was one of them. Sudhir was an ordinary graduate but Vijay's social status was better than his. Sudhir was better in academics, never missed the first class and Vijay had a problem getting through and yet he was more respected than Sudhir. Anything's possible in this country, in this society!

Vijay's father had pampered Vijay a bit too much since he was a child. Vijay suffered from epilepsy and so he was looked after much more. He was a pre-tem baby and his weight was very low. He was kept in the incubator, it seems. Annakaka did everything that this frail son of his asked for and Vijay had an attitude as a child. Annakaka was doing quite alright financially. He held a government job, was corrupt and so made some extra cash on the side. Vijay was a dull student and the only thing that was expected of him was that he clear the academic year. He had passed his school-leaving exam at one go and his father was ecstatic. He threw a big party to celebrate Vijay's success. After two years, Vijay failed another crucial exam and then he was put in a private institution after giving a lot of donation. Vijay never completed his education.

∞ ∞ ∞ ∞ ∞

Sudhir looked at Savni, she seemed to be lost in her own thoughts, seemingly unfocussed. Vijay had a problem with his family because of her. It would have been practical to live in a joint family. Annakaka needed his son after the surgery and Vijay too should have given in. Savni didn't hold a job and Vijay wasn't earning too well. It would have made economic sense for all of them to live together but people, at times, behave so impractically! Don't they understand what's best for them because of their huge egos?

Savni was a very sweet-looking girl. She was fair and a bit overweight. Sudhir would have liked a wife like that but Gayatri seemed to have been his destiny. What was so great about Vijay that he should have found such a pretty wife? What did these things depend on? Your destiny or then how enterprising you are in life? Sudhir was always attracted to Savni. There was no question of sharing this feeling with anybody. He remembered how at a get together in their residential complex they had enacted a scene from a very famous film. Vijay was the hero who was bound by the bad men and Savni had to dance for the evil boss. The minute her feet stopped moving, her man would be killed. The film had become a legend in Indian cinema and this particular sequence, like many in the film, was loved by the audience. So then Vijay, like the hero in the original film, told the heroine, that is Savni, not to dance for the bad dog of a man. Sudhir had suddenly wanted to be the bad man wanted to watch Savni dance for him. It was a cheap fantasy, born out of watching too much of melodrama. Vijay seemed to be still stuck in that age. He also talked like that from time to time, as if he was a hero of some Hindi film.

∞ ∞ ∞ ∞ ∞

Vijay seemed to be searching for someone and after a few minutes couldn't contain himself. "Hasn't she come?" he whispered urgently.

Sudhir didn't get it. Who? His eyebrows rose in confusion. Vijay frowned.

"SHE… Rani…"

"Oh! Rani…" Sudhir remembered.

"Speak softly."

"I had sent her an invite. I'd called her too. If she was to come she should have been here by now. It takes only two hours to reach here from her place."

Rani was his cousin. Her husband worked in a bank and she ran a beauty parlour at home. She was a professional beautician. The girl was always interested in decking up, one always found her looking into the mirror. She was never interested in academics. Her father Vasantkaka had passed away long back. He was a well-known engineer at one point of time and had made a lot of money. They also had a big bungalow but today there was nobody to enjoy living in such a palatial house. Rani had to be married off in a hurry. Her reputation had taken a beating in that small place that they had lived in. Her first affair was with her own cousin, Vijay. It was sort of incestuous. That was the time when Vijay was struggling through his academic career at the polytechnic. Sudhir was in Mumbai then, but these things couldn't be hidden. The whole thing had become a source of spicy gossip. Everybody in the family knew of it. Sudhir was envious. He was as goodlooking as Vijay but he was in a different position, living on people's kindness, an orphan of sorts. So it wasn't easy for him to be able to have fun like Vijay. Vijay was different. He had the looks and he had the social status. He could have girlfriends. He had probably had sex with Rani too. Vijay always considered Sudhir a friend and seemed to be sure that Sudhir would never rat on him. Probably because of his position in the family if nothing else!

So, then, he had discussed Rani with Sudhir. Sudhir remembered how he had once talked of what great fun being with Rani was. There were additional advantages. Rani was the only child and her father had money. So, after marriage the money would be Vijay's. Sudhir had shut up. He knew he would never get what Vijay aimed for. But somehow, Vijay's calculations went wrong. Rani's mother, Vijay's aunt, got her married off to a simple man in some village. He was a timid man and far from being well-off. Rani didn't rebel. She never insisted on marrying Vijay. In fact, she even refused to acknowledge her relationship with him. She told everybody that he was a brother, like all other cousins were. Of course, nobody believed her.

Why did Rani have a fling with Vijay? Just for the fun of it? Or then was it her first real love? She had other boyfriends too, Sudhir had heard of it from his friends. Rani was a sexy girl and her husband was a very simple man. He was probably henpecked. Could Rani have had any more affairs after marriage? She had simply accepted her husband and had gone away to live with him. Such girls sometimes become fiercely loyal to their husbands after marriage, Sudhir had heard. Rani's mother had fallen very ill after her marriage. She was bedridden and had eventually died. Rani was now the owner of a huge property. It would be fun to meet her now, it seemed she talked just like she did earlier, without a care, absolutely nonchalant!

How did Vijay take this whole thing? He had once said, "What's love, after all? There's nothing like love. It's just a word people have coined to delude themselves to glorify their own selfish interests. I love Savni's body. So what if I didn't get Rani? It didn't break me at all. The most important thing is the lust for life and the instinct for self-preservation. We use all the right words to help us survive. Everything else is just a compromise to live."

Vijay's epilepsy seemed to have been cured while in college. He became perfectly normal.

∞ ∞ ∞ ∞ ∞

"Looks like Rani won't turn up," Vijay muttered and Sudhir came back to the present. Why was it happening to him today? Why was he swinging between the past and the present? Just then his eldest aunt came to him.

"Ok, Sudhirrao!" She said lightly. "Time to get married." Sudhir looked at her. She was past 70 and yet looked quite fine. She had lost her husband a year ago but her face didn't show any of that pain. That's actually such a good thing. But in our society, a woman is supposed to break down and never recover once she's widowed. His aunt herself was of that opinion when her husband was alive. She followed him everywhere like his shadow. Her husband, Sudhir's uncle, was a highly-placed officer in the Forest Department. He had a wonderful personality, intimidating too, and a voice that matched his looks. His son, Prakash, was the only child. When he couldn't get into a medical or an engineering college, uncle had thrown a fit – like it was a horrible crime committed by the government in not letting the boy into a medical college; like the family had suffered a grave calamity.

Prakash was a bright boy and everybody had hoped he would become a doctor but he disappointed his family. He did his Masters in Science and then took up a government job. His wife, Kiran, was a very ambitious woman and hated her husband's lack of ambition. Had he got into the private sector, he would have made a lot of money, she always felt. Prakash didn't care.

The same uncle, who had thrown a fit when Prakash couldn't secure an admission in a medical or engineering college, had made the decision of making Sudhir join a simple commerce college. Sudhir wanted to study engineering, he had got a good grade and he could have secured an admission where he wanted. But he couldn't tell that to anybody, bent as he was under the obligations of his uncles and aunts. He was close to his cousins, but not close enough to express his ambitions to any of them. He lived with Annakaka at that time and all the decisions about him were taken by his uncles collectively. People were never bothered or eager to know his results. He would pass, that was about it.

Neither was his own mother bothered about him. She had once sent him a letter wishing him Good Luck for the exam. When he went to spend the holidays with her, she didn't ask him about his future plans, of how he wanted his career to shape up. Instead she complained about how the tenents didn't pay regularly, how the government officials troubled etc. Of course, she too had nobody to share her life with. But Sudhir was too young to be interested in her talk and he was irritated with her for not having had any interest in listening to him.

Sudhir had lost his childhood before time. He had matured prematurely, so to say. Nobody was bad to him at his uncles' homes. Nobody troubled him, nobody was rude. He ate good food, was not treated badly and yet there was no real affection for him. Bringing him up was more out of a sense of duty. His home changed after every two-three years when he was shifted from one uncle to another. He didn't have a choice. Nobody asked him what he thought of it. His mother was considered to be useless and incapable of bringing him up. She didn't bother to prove them wrong. In fact, it boosted this view of her by walking out of the house and living by herself in her mother's home. Everybody had hated her at her husband's place. She was considered inauspicious because her husband had cancer. In reality, he had got cancer after seven-eight years of marriage. Then how was it her fault? But, apparently, her horoscope said that she would bring about her husband's death. Annakaka was supposed to have married her. He was a little older than Sudhir's father. The horoscopes were matched and she was to marry Annakaka but then somebody in the family talked of how there was a problem. The horoscope was checked again by another astrologer who suggested that Annakaka not marry the girl. The match was broken. Sudhir could imagine how his mother felt at that time.

Then his father came forth and announced that horoscopes were humbug and that he would marry the girl. He ignored everybody's protests and married her and brought her into the family. The elders in the family believed till the very end that it was because of her planetary position that his father had diesd of cancer. That was the time man had already landed on the moon! His mother was termed inauspicious and simply shifted Sudhir's responsibility on the family that branded her unlucky and it accepted it grudgingly.

The eldest uncle had written to her after Sudhir's school-leaving exams, "It would be best if he studied humanities or then commerce. The cost of studying science would be too high. If he got into the engineering college, who was to bear all that cost? It was best to avoid all those problems." The letter also said, "Let him finish his graduation and get a degree. After that his destiny will take him wherever he's to go. If he gets a job in a bank, his life will be made." When his uncle had shown him the letter Sudhir had felt weepy but couldn't possibly have shown his emotions. He had had a sudden urge to run away to his mother. Tell her that he wanted to study science, that she should look after him, help him make the decisions that he wanted to make in life. But his voice wouldn't have reached that woman. She was uneducated herself, had no energy for life, no zest to live it any other way that the way she did. How could he shake her out of her stupor? He couldn't possibly have rebelled. While sending him to his uncles his mother had told him, "Don't ask for anything. Just accept whatever comes your way. You are a dependent. You will have no say and it's best to kill all your desires and aspirations before they are vocalised."

Sudhir didn't know how much of this advice he had grasped but he seemed to have followed it. His uncles always patted his back for being understanding and being mature beyond his years. "He's aware that he is a fatherless boy." They said. Yes, Sudhir knew what being fatherless was.

When Sudhir got into a commerce college, his cousins were already in the science colleges. There was now no question of being compared with them. Rani was slightly older than him, a few months younger to Vijay. There was no question of being compared with her for anything.

The eldest uncle was very smart. He made sure that Sudhir was never kept in his house. He always adviced his brothers of how to shift him around. He was older than the other brothers and so all of them followed his advice. That was the way things were in the family. So the eldest uncle saw to it that Sudhir was everybody else's responsibility other than his own.

∞ ∞ ∞ ∞ ∞

Sudhir stood in front of the priest for the actual ceremony. Beyond the veil was Gayatri. He felt nothing. No excitement, no happiness, nothing special. Did it happen when one crossed over to the late 30s in life? Had his mind too lost its freshness? He had waited for so long and then had ended up marrying a woman like Gayatri.

He never felt excited looking at her. He was marrying her because he didn't want to die single. He had been looking for a wife for so long. It had to stop somewhere.

Finally the vows were taken. Sudhir noticed that a lot of his relatives had made it to the ceremony. He was sure everybody had heaved a sigh of relief. Sudhir was getting married, at last!

The other rituals continued. Gayatri's mother had insisted that they be completed. Sudhir wasn't too keen, but his family too was quite religious. They were a known family at one point of time. His grandfather was a highly-respected doctor, the family was very well off. His grandfather had built a big bungalow, lived there for a year or two and then passed away in his sleep. That was just before Sudhir was born. His uncles and aunts got married and moved away and his grandmother remained in that big bungalow with his father and uncle Arun, Arunkaka. Arunkaka didn't study much, he didn't even finish school. He somehow got into a government job with somebody's help and then stuck on till he retired. Sudhir's father was in the Agriculture department of the government. During holidays the entire family got together. Sudhir remembered how particular everybody was about the holy rituals, of how nobody touched the meal without saying their prayers first.

Sudhir found himself following the traditions but then he also saw how the people who prayed so hard behaved otherwise in their lives and he lost his faith in God. He got quite sure of the fact that those who were obsessed with God were downright hypocrites. His eldest uncle was a good example of it. When his grandmother passed away the brothers decided to divide the property amongst themselves.

It was unnecessary. Arunkaka lived there, the bungalow was huge and there were tenents. The rent supported Arunkaka's life. Eldest uncle had lived in government quarters all his life and now after retirement needed a house to live in. So he decided that the bungalow had to be sold off. He also announced that the sisters didn't need any money, they could be given a tiny amount as a token. He also announced that he had spent for the education of all the younger brothers and that is why had no time to save up anything for himself. The others were stunned. When did he spend on their education? They couldn't remember. "Our mother knew it," he said. She was dead. There was no one who could challenge this. He decided that the youngest uncle and Annakaka had enough of their own, so they didn't need any money, some money had to be kept for Sudhir's future and some had to be given to Arunkaka to buy another house. The rest, he kept for himself. Nobody said a thing against him and signed the papers. Sudhir had heard some murmurs of protests in the family but they didn't reach

the eldest uncle. Sudhir himself was in no position to talk about anything. He was very young and the fact that the uncles brought him up was a huge obligation. The bungalow got sold and Arunkaka said that the new house would be too small and he had two children who were growing up. He couldn't accommodate Sudhir anymore. Sudhir was shifted to Annakaka's house in Mumbai.

The bungalow was sold off and Sudhir hardly ever went back to the family place again except for once when out of some inexplicable desire he reached what used to be his grandfather's bungalow. It was now dilapidated. Sudhir wandered around the desolate and abandoned dwelling. It never belonged to him but it gave him a sense of belonging. It brought people together though only for appearances sake, at least once or twice a year, and then it had a festive appearance with the entire family buzzing about. There were uncles, aunts, cousins. People talking laughing, kids playing for sometime atleast everyone forgot their differences, envies and wraths. One felt full of life, and life felt full of happiness. Sudhir felt so proud to be a part of that illustrious family! But then, when the bungalow broke down, so did the delicate strings that kept the family together. There was no need for anybody to gather at one place. Festivals were celebrated individually, the family members wandered away from each other.

The next time Sudhir went there, there was no bungalow, no trace of it at all. Instead there stood an apartment complex. New building, new people. Sudhir felt stirred by nostalgia and emotion. Did familial relationships really mean anything even when the bungalow stood in its place? Or was it all as easy to break down as a structure of bricks and mortar? What were relationships all about anyway? Did they really mean anything to anybody in today world?

The eldest uncle was supposed to be a religious man. He spent a lot of time going through religious rituals, visited temples often. One felt better in the serenity of the temple where his rituals were on. But then why didn't the man's goodness extend to the people around him? He took most of the money for himself, he decided on the direction of Sudhir's life without asking for his opinion. Was he a good man? Did his rituals mean anything? What virtue did that man have despite being so pious?

∞ ∞ ∞ ∞ ∞

Sudhir's mind was elsewhere but his body went through the rituals. His uncle and aunt sat next to him where traditionally the parents needed to sit. His mother couldn't sit by herself. She couldn't play the role of both the father and mother during the ceremony. Religion didn't permit it. What kind of traditions were these? What if he had insisted on his mother being there, by herself? Would the priests have agreed to it? And, most importantly, would his mother have agreed to something like this? Would she have supported his decision? His mother had never stood by him, never made any decisions. She only agreed with everything and everybody and simply went with the flow.

Sudhir looked at Annakaka sitting next to him. He too was a religious man. In less than two years, he got Sudhir out of the house under the pretext of keeping him away from bad company, the bad company being his own son Vijay. His wife, too, told everybody that she didn't want a fatherless son to ruin his life because of her son. Vijay wanted to be a film star. The fact was that they didn't want him in the house. He scored good marks while Vijay flunked. The comparison was obvious. They couldn't take it anymore. They told the younger uncle that it would have been easier for Sudhir to commute from his place rather than their's. Younger uncle didn't refuse. Sudhir spent the final years of his academic life at the younger uncle's place. He had looked after Sudhir fairly well.

Why hadn't younger uncle come for the wedding? He wouldn't have missed Sudhir's wedding. He was irritated when he had got nothing when the property was divided. "Is it a sin to be doing well? Why shouldn't I get anything from my father's property? He," he said of the eldest brother, "didn't spend anything on me. I studied on scholarships. He himself was in a good job. Why didn't he save up enough to buy a house? The man is a liar." But he never said this openly. Later on, he was also upset with Annakaka. There was a reason. He had a vacant flat which a man who was Annakaka's acquaintance, had rented. The man later, not only didn't pay the rent, he even refused to move out. When Younger uncle tried to get Annakaka into the matter, he was unpleasantly surprised. Annakaka simply refused to have anything to do with the whole matter. "I wasn't getting the rent of the place. If you gained, the losses will also be your's," he had said matter of factly.

Annakaka need not have behaved like that. It was his moral responsibility because the culprit was an acquaintance of his. But he refused to acknowledge his responsibility and the issue went to the court. Finally, after a couple of years, the tenent was thrown out but the younger uncle didn't forget Annakaka's indifference. He was angry.

Annakaka was an angry man too. But he was angry with the eldest uncle. He hadn't got anything from his father's property either. "Who's he to decide whether we need the money or not? So what if he's the eldest and was born before all of us? Is that some sort of a virtue? Why should we listen to him?" he was heard saying. Sudhir believed all of them.

∞ ∞ ∞ ∞ ∞

It was time for lunch. People started eating. Tradition demanded that the bride and the groom go to each table and encourage people to eat more and more, at times, serve the dessert themselves. In reality it didn't seem plausible. The waiters who served didn't even wait for anybody to say either Yes or No. They moved with such speed that people could barely stop them. Those who were shy would get up on an empty stomach. Sudhir suddenly noticed youngest uncle and his wife with his aunt Pratima's son Raghav and his wife. Sudhir rushed to them.

"What took you so long?"

"The traffic jam was unbelievable. And do people in your city ever give the right address?" Raghav winked. He looked so good despite the journey!

Raghav was a gem of a man. He always had a smile on his face, everybody loved him. He was a successful businessman. He had studied to be an engineer and then did his Masters in Business Administration. He was the first among the cousins to have his own business. He had left the job-holders far behind.

"How's Pratimaatya?" Sudhir enquired after his aunt.

"Just the way she is. Can she ever improve?" Raghav laughed. That laughter hid pain. Sudhir had realised it when he had gone to meet his aunt and invite them for the wedding. He hadn't seen his aunt for a long time and had heard that she was bed-ridden. He was shaken up when he saw her. She was a ghost of her earlier self. He had known her as a dynamic woman. After her husband died, she fell ill. She was the only one who didn't do too well all her life. Her husband had an ordinary job and had become an officer at the fag end of his career. He didn't have much of a standing in the family. He was also the least favoured son-in-law. Money evokes respect and he had no money, so he didn't have much of respect either. Pratimaatya's sisters were well-placed and yet shea didn't lose her morale. She brought up her children, Raghav and Usha, very well. Both the children studied well, Usha got married and went off to the US. Raghav turned out to be very enterprising. Times changed and then he became the richest among the cousins. He was blessed by both, the goddess of money and wisdom.

Sudhir met Raghav after he met his aunt and then a new emotion opend up to him. Raghav had spoken his heart out. "My mother and I are miles apart emotionally," he had said. "I'm really grateful to her for the way she brought us up. She took a lot of pains to give me good education and our financial situation improved only after I started working. My father passed away just when I had started my business. Today, I can give her every comfort but she doesn't seem to be in a position to enjoy it. After my father's death, she's always been ill. After my sister's wedding all her responsibilities have ended. Even today she eats well, gets jewellery made but we have no connection whatsoever. One or twice a day I ask her how she is. Rest of the times, I'm busy and she's in her own room. She does have heart ailments and some neurological problems and I've taken her to the best of the doctors, but her problem is not physical, it's psychological. It's as if she feels that only if she remains ill will I pay any attention to her. She's not interested in reading or television. Her life was the kitchen which she feels has been taken over by my wife. I want to take her on vacations with the family but she's always so insecure, so very much in her own world. My wife takes very good care of her, cleans her toilet at times, and yet she shouts at her, bullies her. No attendant sticks around because of her behaviour. She abuses them. It's only my good luck that my wife hasn't left me as yet. I've won everywhere in life but I've lost as far as my mother is concerned. I just want her to go now. What's the use of a life that is spent in bed all the 24 hours? Sometimes she gets up and then has a fall. The last time she fell, she hurt her head real bad. She had to be admitted in the hospital. My mother has done a lot for me but now I want her to go. The stress is intolerable." Raghav had spoken for a long time. What he said was killing him, it was obvious. What kind of a relationship was that where one wanted one's own mother to die?

"We are sentimental people," Raghav was saying. "We always weep for the dead. But how much should a person live? If someone dies young, one can understand. But how much can one mourn a very old person? It's like calling the commercial mourners at somebody's death. I am grateful to my mother but does it mean that I would want her to continue to live in this condition? Death is liberating many times. It's just another law of nature. All of us are to go one day or the other."

Raghav was a philosopher of sorts. He looked at life seriously and Sudhir always liked to talk to him.

∞ ∞ ∞ ∞ ∞

"Why don't all of you have lunch now? I'm sure you are tired." Sudhir said.

"That's ok, a little while later…Let's meet everybody first. Where's your mother? Today's her day too," younger uncle said lightly. He had a subtle sense of humour and he was often the heart of a party. And then he came to Sudhir and asked, "Has Shakuntala come?" Shakuntala was his own sister.

"No, only her husband is here."

"She wouldn't dare to face me. Had she been here today, I would have insulted her in front of the whole family…" younger uncle's tone suddenly changed. It had been 10 years since his daughter had eloped with Shakuntalaatya's son. He hadn't forgotten. He had once said, "Shakuntala is being arrogant because she has all three sons. But now she has granddaughters too. Let one of them run away from home with a man, only then will she know how it feels. I'll never forgive her."

It was serious. Shakuntalaatya's son, Niranjan, had stayed at younger uncle's place to study his Master's in Business Administration and had fallen in love with Suman, younger uncle's daughter. Things were heating up and all other cousins knew about it. Suman's mother knew it too but didn't take it seriously and one day, on the last day of her BA exams, after the paper, Suman simply eloped with Niranjan to get married. Niranjan's parents had supported them all along. Younger uncle felt betrayed. Shakuntalaatya said later that it was necessary to do things this way. Had they sent a formal marriage proposal to Suman, her parants wouldn't have agreed to it. Suman knew her parants, her mother was very strict and would never have accepted Niranjan as a son- in-law. They would have, instead, got her married off to somebody hastily.

The family was shaken up by this incident. Nobody would have expected Niranjan to behave like this and Suman to support him. This was dramatic, just like in Hindi films. Sudhir was at Tingri at that time and had come to know about this after a long time. Younger uncle had sent him a letter. He had written to all the members of the family appealing to them to not keep in touch with Shakuntalastya's family. He also cursed them and said that Shakuntalaatya's family would never do well in life. But that didn't seem to have happened. Her family thrived and flourished. Looked like younger uncle's curse didn't have much of a power. Or then was it because in the modern world people who behave wrongly thrive? Sudhir remembered how while he had stayed with him, he had asked his uncle if he could study further do his post-graduation. Uncle was frank. "It's difficult, Sudhir," he said. "If somebody else is to take your responsibility, then it's alright but I can't do it. Suman has almost completed her education, she has to be married off and Niranjan wants to come and stay with us too. It's not possible for me to look after both of you."

Sudhir understood. He had never viewed Suman sexually. For him, she was always a cousin sister. Then how could Niranjan feel attracted to her? Wasn't it incestuous? Sudhir too had felt attracted to Rani. Was what Vijay said true? Was the only relationship that existed between a man and a woman sexual? Why did people marry? Only to have a partner to have sex? Why did he want a beautiful wife? Why did younger uncle find it more important to pay for Niranjan's education rather than his? It was awkward for Sudhir to ask any other uncle to pay for his education. His mother was also keen that he start working. She wanted to live with him. Sudhir became a clark in a bank and got stuck in the mediocre job.

It was good that Shakuntalaatya didn't attend the wedding or else there would have been unpleasantness. Sudhir didn't know whose side he was on. Other than younger uncle everybody was on good terms with Shakuntalaatya's family. Nobody cared for uncle's appeal. People were even secretly happy about what had happened. Uncle had fewer problems than others and the family thought that he was smug. Annakaka had, in fact, said, "What can others do if he couldn't take care of his own daughter?" He held Suman more guilty than anybody else. Younger uncle was very hurt that nobody else cared for his appeal to alienate Shakuntalaatya's family.

"Nobody cares! Girls are being kidnapped in the broad daylight and nobody's bothered! What's wrong with all of you?" his letter was dramatic. Nobody had any response to it. When Sudhir had met the eldest uncle, he had said, "Why should we break our contacts with Shakuntala for somebody? If she is bad, does it make him good?' "Who is good?" Sudhir wanted to ask him. All of them had clay feet. Only Arunkaka had stood by younger uncle. Younger uncle and Annakaka had helped him a lot during a medical emergency and he probably felt a sense of loyalty. That was for two years but after that slowly he mended relations with Shakuntalaatya's family.His children took the initiative and later the parents had followed.

Arunkaka wasn't without pain either. His son Kishore was disabled because of a polio-afflicted leg. He was very bright but the pain of his disability was a lot for Arunkaka to bear. Both Annakaka and younger uncle had helped him in Kishore's case a lot and he was grateful to them. That gratitude made him respond to younger uncle's appeal to sever contacts with Shakuntalaatya's family. Younger uncle was deeply affected by the Suman episode. He felt humiliated and gradually withdrew from public functions and even from his own family. He was hardly ever seen. It was a big thing that he had attended the wedding.

The groom's side sat down for lunch. There was eldest uncle's wife, her son Prakash, his wife Kiran and their daughter Mugdha. Then Annakaka, his wife, Vijay-Savni and their kids. Sudhir couldn't recall the children's names. People hardly ever visited each other and he was in the faraway Tingri for many years. The issue of his marriage had become a joke. He didn't feel like being the source of entertainment and so had stopped visiting people. In any case, nobody had really cared for him. He was a man who had been brought up by other people. But today was different. He was sitting amongst his own family, his wife and his mother. Everybody else had come to celebrate what was essentially his day.

Next to Annakaka was Arunkaka, his wife, son Kishore. His daughter, Asmita wasn't here. Her exams were on. Next to him were younger uncle and his wife. Their son Mangesh was very bright and also a well-behaved boy. Then there was Raghav, his wife who was a doctor and their son. There was no question of Pratimaatya being able to attend the function. Raghav's wife was said to be a very fine lady. Everybody praised her for her softspokenness and the way she looked after her ailing mother-in-law.

There weren't too many people from the eldest aunt's family. Rani hadn't turned up. She hadn't care much about her breakup with Vijay. Usually she attended all the family functions and gossiped about those who didn't. She loved to gossip. Why hadn't she come? Did she know that Vijay would be here? Was that the reason?

In a way it was a good thing. Or else, thought Sudhir, he would have thought more of her than Gayatri. She had already ruined a lot of his nights.

Shakuntalaatya's husband Narharkaka was around. It was obvious that he was there only for the sake of formality. Formality! Everybody had attended the wedding of a man who was dependent on them at one time, only to be socially correct. It was a formality.

His mother's family was there too. She had six sisters. All of them did well in life but Sudhir was never really in touch with them. He had grown up at his uncles' and had always stayed with his mother during the holidays. Nobody was interested in spending their holidays in the small town where his mother had lived. Neither did Sudhir and his mother visit anybody. It was probably an inferiority complex that stopped them from staying at the homes of people who were better off than them. Two of his aunts lived in the same city when he was in Mumbai but he stopped visiting them. Whenever they saw him they always cursed his father's family and he didn't really like it. Later he had gone to Tingri. Who had time for relatives and their talk?

Sudhir himself was slowly moving away from his father's family. His mother was happy that her family was present in its full strength for the function. Her only son was getting married. She received each of them personally. Sudhir was formal. He never felt a part of them. Everybody's tales of happiness were the same and that of pain were different. His mother's family always looked happy. He had never tried to peep into their lives and see the reality for the fear of coming across an unpleasant surprise. Nobody at that function looked unhappy. People wore bright, expensive clothes, jewellery, looked good. How many of them were really happy? And why was he thinking about the possible grief that they might have had? What was wrong with him? It was his wedding day. His mind was supposed to have healed and yet all he could feel was the wound, reopened and bleeding.

"Sing a short couplet for your wife, something really funny," Kiran said to him. He was surprised that she should say this to him. Eldest uncle had thrown her out of the house. He and his wife were both very religious, to the point of being obsessed with God. Kiran was agnostic. It was rare to find women who didn't believe in God. They had arguments over the issue all the time. For Prakash, it was a difficult situation. Uncle also abused his daughter-in-law. He was a crude man despite all that religious fervour and had lived his entire life in a jungle. He was with the Forest department. There was no scope for any finesse in personality. Kiran had left the house one day and Prakash had no choice but to follow her. For two years they lived away from his parents and then had got back. Uncle had made peace with them. But things hadn't really changed. Whenever one went to their home, both the parties complained about each other in low voices. One could feel the tension. Sudhir never understood what Prakash's role in the whole issue was. He preferred to spend more time at his office. Kiran talked against her husband even to outsiders. She wanted him to work in the private sector, and Savni wanted her husband to be a businessman. Vijay earned well in the private sector. Why weren't women happy with their husbands? Why didn't they recognise the real caliber of their husbands? Everybody wanted more and more. Was it, in any way, related to sex? Because men didn't satisfy their wives that they remained dissatisfied in other areans as well? Sudhir didn't understand the complexity of a husband-wife relationship. But he was getting married, finally.

There didn't seem any problems between Raghav and his wife Anagha. She never critisized him. Were they compatible? Or was the reality completely different? Anagha was always very calm, satisfied. Raghav talked a lot, a bit too much. This couple was probably more of an exception than a rule. Most couples were like Prakash and Kiran, living together because they had to. Where would his marriage take him? He was getting into a relationship at 36, and wasn't too sure of it.

∞ ∞ ∞ ∞ ∞

Sudhir made up a great couplet for his wife which meant that he should get Gayatri for the next seven births. Gayatri too said something similar. Both of then fed each other.

Sudhir looked at Kishore. He too should have got married by now. He was handicapped but very bright. In fact, he was the one who suggested a good couplet to Sudhir. Once he had said, "I don't want a job in the quota reserved for the handicapped. I want to find a job like everybody else, in an open category." He worked for two years in the private sector but then found the strain on his legs unbearable when he had to spend hours on the site of work. In the private sector nobody give any special concessions. He was then forced to find a government job by mentioning his handicap. "In a way I am the government's son-in-law," he used to joke. But it rose out of pain. When Sudhir had gone

to invite him for the wedding he had said, "I will marry only a handicapped girl. I don't care what kind of handicap she has. We'll support each other." Sudhir prayed fervently that Kishor find a wonderful partner."

Narharkaka was the only representative of the older sons-in-law. Pratimaatya had lost her husband, eldest aunt and her husband were both dead. Sudhir had heard that Narharkaka had had an affair with Arunkaka's wife, Ashakaku, many years back. He was in school at that time. Arunkaka was furious. He wanted to kill Narharkaka and Sudhir's grandmother had stopped him. Arunkaka was a short-tempered man. His wife seemed like a very quiet woman. It was impossible to understand people. Narharkaka didn't come home for many years after that. Nobody talked of it but the affair was a serious. Was one of Arunkaka's children actually Narharkaka's? Sudhir was friends with all the three boys. Not one of them attended his wedding. Blood relations spoiled friendship.

∞ ∞ ∞ ∞ ∞

Lunch was done. People started going away. There was no function in the evening. Sudhir started his Thank Yous. The eldest aunt hugged him. "We aren't going to be around for too long, son," she said. "You will have to maintain the relationships in future. Till we are alive all of us will meet somehow or the other. It shouldn't happen that all of you move away after we are gone. Be close to your family."

After her husband passed away the eldest aunt had picked up the pieces of her life quite well. It had been two years since his death. She lived well. How did she manage it? Pratimaatya was just the opposite. She was bed-ridden after her husband passed away. Her daughter-in-law was a good woman. Anybody else in her place would have left home by now.

"One hardly meets relatives these days because of this city life, If you live in two different suburbs, it seems as if one lives in two different cities. Life has become too fast and the struggle for survival seems to take up most of your time. People have become so self-centered. How do we meet each other?" younger uncle joined in the conversation.

"Today there are single child families. How would the future generations even understand what relationships are all about? People live alone, go through life all by themselves…" Annakaka usually didn't participate in discussions but he seemed to have got into the mood. Then everybody joined them.

What were relationships? When we feel close to somebody, a relationship is formed. At times, some relations defy definition. How many of our blood relations are we close to? How many of them do we miss if we don't meet them for some time? How many do we bother to even write an occasional letter to? Wasn't there anybody here who would fit the description? Sudhir thought. There isn't anybody in my life who I can't live without. How did I live for 35 years without anybody? How did I survive amidst relationships that were based on formality? Why did the uncles bring me up? Was it because it would have been socially incorrect to abandon me or did they really feel some affection for a fatherless boy?

What was happening to him today? Sudhir wondered. More and more layers of existence were being peeled off on his wedding day. Man is selfish by nature. He lives for himself and creates relationships for himself. Once his need is over, relationships are over too. Today he was trying to form the best relationship in his life. A delicate, soft, loving association with Gayatri. Why did the meaning of other relationships reach his mind at the same time?

"Now when do we meet again?" somebody asked.

"When someone dies or then for yet another wedding," Raghav was brutally honest. It seemed inappropriate to discuss possible deaths and so people discussed possible weddings in the family in the near future.

Then all of them started leaving. Nobody was to stay back. In the earlier times people stayed for a week after the wedding. Today nobody was interested. Each one wanted to get back into their own space.

It was evening. Sudhir had made rounds of various temples, as the tradition demanded. He wasn't interested in it but didn't argue. He decided to slowly talk about it with Gayatri. Her parents were with them and so was his mother. Gayatri's parents had two apartments in the city and had some savings. Gayatri was the only child and so all of it would eventually belong to him. He knew of all this before marrying her. So had he married money? He had taken care of his own interests while marrying her.

They visited all the possible temples and then Gayatri's parents came to reach them home. Sudhir's aunt, Vidulamavshi was waiting for them at home. She had lost her husband recently.

"We'll have the special rituals tomorrow. Please come over. And also take care of our daughter. Tomorrow you can leave for your honeymoon. You might need to do all the packing for it tonight," Gayatri's father said. Suddenly Gayatri broke into a sob. She hugged her mother and cried more. Her mother patted her with affection.

"We have brought her up with velvet gloves. We're sure you'll look after her well," her mother said. Slowly Gayatri's sobs subsided. After a while her parents left with a heavy heart. Now there were only four people in the house: Sudhir, his mother, Gayatri and Sudhir's aunt. According to the tradition, the couple couldn't have sex on the wedding night. It was only after some more rituals the next morning that they could come together. The thought suddenly became unbearable for Sudhir. He had waited to touch a woman for so long. He had remained a virgin for 35 long years, He had had enough of the formalities.

"She will sleep in my room tonight," he snapped.

His mother started. Gayatri's downcast face hid her embarrassment.

"What will people say if they get to know of this? You've waited for so long. Why not wait for another night?" his mother asked. "When you go on your honeymoon, she's all yours."

"It's your responsibility to not let the people know. And even if they do, I don't care. She's my wife."

"Why not ask her?" his mother said and Gayatri blushed. Sudhir looked at Gayatri. He couldn't believe that modern women could blush.

"Let's go into the bedroom," he said to her and looked at his mother. His own mother. What association did he have with the woman, a relationship that never matured? He didn't even have a real relationship with his own mother. Both of them were alone in their own way, they could have stood by each other. But his mother had shirked her responsibility. How easily she left him to be brought up by others! She played no role in his life. He had had an argument with her the previous night. None of his uncles and aunts had come for the pre-wedding rituals and finally, his mother's sister and her husband officiated as his godparents.

The whole issue irritated Sudhir. He confronted his mother. "All this wouldn't have happened had you brought me up," he shouted. "I have doubled under the weight of gratitude of my uncles and I'll have to live with it for the rest of my life. All this is thanks to you!"

"They haven't done you any favour. They were only trying to wash away their brother's sins," she said.

"What do you mean? What did my father do?" This was something new.

"Are you ready to hear it a day before your wedding? " Sudhir suddenly felt suffocated. What was she going to say?

"One of the brothers had rejected me because I was inauspicious for my husband's health and the other brother got me home. That was because he wanted somebody who was timid and would feel grateful to him for marrying her. I was just that. Your father was a womanizer. He had relationships with other women even before he married me. Then Pama came into his life. She was the first female engineer in that part of the State. She was Narharkaka's niece. Their association defied logic and both of them openly romanced in front of me. When you were born, your father didn't even bother to see you. He had gone on a holiday with Pama. The entire family knew it but nobody said anything. I was the only one who suffered in the process. I don't know what would have happed later, whether he would have left me for Pama. But he had cancer and she dumped him and married another man. Your father died as my husband. Life of a widow is better than that of a woman who has been discarded by her husband. People were sympathetic and the family decided to take moral responsibility of looking after you. They didn't want me, but they wanted you. I'm a very ordinary woman. Is being ordinary a crime? Your father never made me happy. His memory remained with me in your form. I never felt like bringing you up. You were the result of a life with him. I never got along with him. What I got from my marriage was only stress. I don't know how different life would have been had I decided to bring you up." She was very calm.

"Why didn't I come to know about it ever?"

"Who would tell you? Had I done what your father had done, they would have torn me to shreds. No relationship which is genuine."

Sudhir found his eyes filling up with tears. For the first time in his life he cried openly. For once, he felt close to his mother.

∞ ∞ ∞ ∞ ∞

Sudhir went to his room with Gayatri. Today, he had checked out all the possible relationships between a so-called family. Now came the most important relationship in his life. Both of them were tired. They lay down on the bed.

"Are you tired?" he asked her.

"Yes, you look tired too."

"Yes."

"Did you want me tonight itself?" she asked him boldly.

"Yes."

"Can I ask you something?"

"Go ahead."

"Would this be your first experience?"

Sudhir was stunned. His wife was bold. Probably modern women were like that. He didn't know.

"Yes," he said.

"So, you are eager to experience it, then?"

"Yes."

"I'm proud of you. You've kept your body chaste even at this age. Will you be upset if I told you something?"

"What?"

"You seem to be understanding.If I don't tell you, you might not even know but later on come to know about it in a distorted form from outsiders. I want to start a new association on a clean slate, honestly. You might want to know why I didn't tell you this before marriage. I didn't, because otherwise you wouldn't have married me."

"What do you mean?"

"Will you hear me out without losing your temper?"

Sudhir didn't have a choice but to say Yes.

"I was past 30. I am educated and have a good job, my father has some money but I'm aware that I'm far from attractive. I didn't have any standing in the marriage market. I had friends in the bank, one of them was a man called Joshi.

Sudhir stiffened.

"Joshi was married and was in his 40s. He was very goodlooking. About two years back during an office picnic at the dam close by, while generally having fun, he touched me accidently and I felt myself getting aroused.

He felt it and pulled me in his arms. I didn't protest. I needed sex too. Nobody else noticed us.

'I want you,' he said. I couldn't think straight. As if I gave myself to him. Nothing happened and we returned home.

After a few days he told me that his wife was going away for a few days and that I should visit him at his place. He took it for granted that I would do as he said. I knew where he lived. I knew his wife. I went to his house and we chatted for a while. He made me feel comfortable and then we had sex. He had, of course, taken precaution. I felt sated. I didn't think I would ever get a husband. Too many men had rejected me. Somebody had accepted my body. This happened a couple of times. We should have maintained some self-control but we didn't. He was senior to me. One day he told me that somebody had seen me with him. His wife had suspected. He got himself transferred to another branch. It was all over. That's it. I wanted to tell you this. I don't know why you chose to marry me. It could be probably because I will inherit my parents' money, or because I have a good job. Nobody really cares for emotions these days, do they? It seems like an impossible task in today's world. I want to be honest with you and so shared this. I will always remain faithful to you."

Gayatri was tired. She closed her eyes. Sudhir had heard her out. He felt strange. For a moment he wanted to get up and give her a hard slap. He wanted to shout at her and say, "You've cheated me." But then he understood the uselessness of it all. Life seemed to be like that. He would have to start a new relationship on a new note. He held her close and said, "I want you."

A
B
C
D
E
210 Gaks
70
60
40
40
Nive. 3
Nivel 2
Niv. 2
Niv. 1
Base
60
70 Gaks
50
70
A57-3122.6 Gas
August 2016
CENTRI-SPEWGE
0 15 30 60

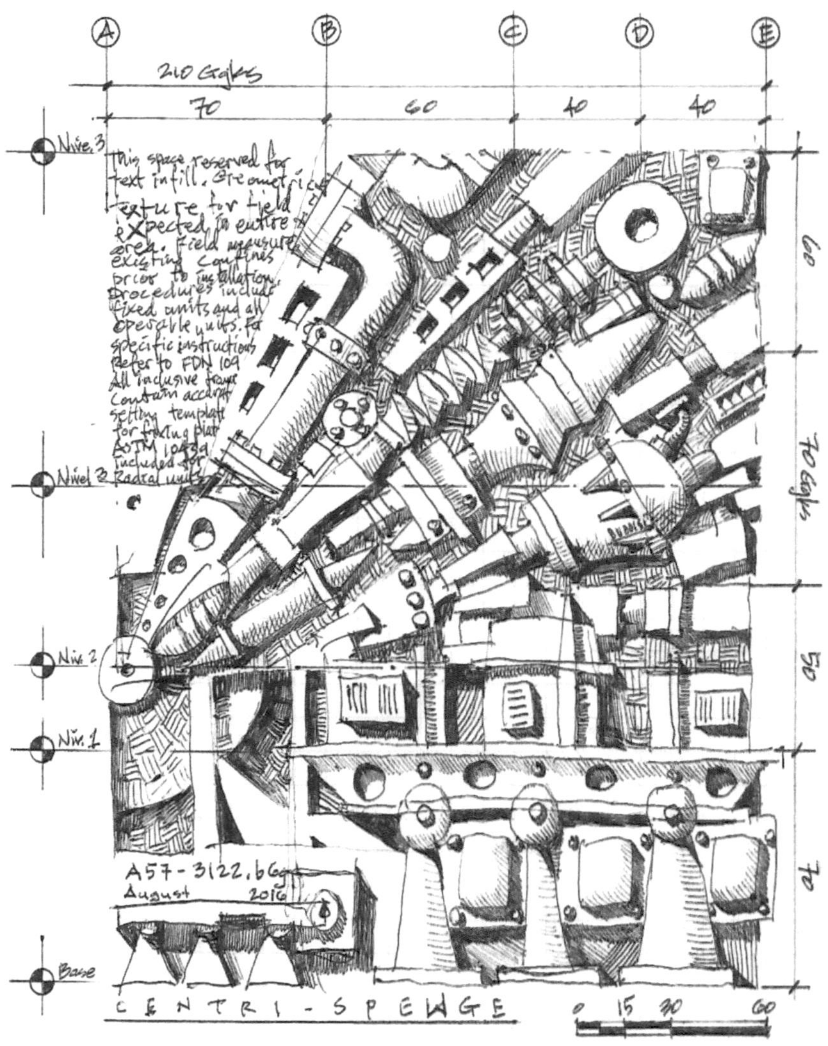

By Floater

The Train Ride

By

John Galgay

Barry Grant loved trains. He had loved their majestic size, their haunting whistle, their straight lines ever since he could remember. Specifically, it was when Barry was three that he saw his first train up close.

David Grant, Barry's father, had been promoted and transferred to the Indianapolis home office of the Providers Insurance Company. David's commute from Pekesville, where they lived, meant taking the 45-minute train ride into the city. In order to surprise her husband after his first day at his new job, Jessica Grant put little Barry in the car seat and drove over to the Pekesville Train Depot.

Pekesville Depot was a rather huge station for its suburban location. It was the service station for the Indiana-Pacific Railroad. The trains were checked out and repaired here before heading to Indianapolis for routes south and west.

Jessica was going to sit in the parking lot and wait for David. However, little Barry listened to the brakes hiss and metal scraping against metal and insisted on a closer look. He pleaded, "Mommy, can I see the choo-choos?"

She tried to dismiss him with, "The trains are too loud. They'll frighten you. Let's wait here for Daddy." Always observant of his mother's rule, Barry desisted. He just peered out the window at the mighty engines.

The 5:14 slid into Pekesville right on schedule. David was drifting towards his car when he heard Jessica's loving voice call out to him. David raced up to her and gave her a big hug. After his bewildering day in the big city, he was glad his family had come to meet him. He leaned into his wife's car to kiss his son. "How's Daddy's biggest boy?"

He usually got the impressive sardonic retort; "I'm your only boy, Daddy." This time, Barry stared right past his father and whined, "Mommy won't let me see the trains."

He appeased his son with a non-committal, "Just hold on there, big guy."

Careful of his wife's wrath, he asked Jessica why his son couldn't see the trains. Upon hearing the reason was their loudness, he laughed, reached into the car, and scooped Barry into his arms asking, "Those trains aren't too loud for Big Barry, are they?"

"No, Daddy."

Obviously miffed at this defeat in child rearing, Jessica said curtly, "Aunt Jane is coming to supper tonight. Don't be long. I'll see you at home." At that, she rushed off in her Dodge Dart.

David thought as he capered (that odd gait large men must take while holding hands with a small running child) towards the station, having achieved a rare male victory for the Grant men, this tour would be a good one.

David had ridden the trains many times but had never bothered to notice them. Now, he looked through his son's eyes. He saw their strength and hard beauty. He was asked how those precarious (not the word Barry used) little wheels stayed on the narrow tracks. He was also asked how far the tracks went and if they were the same distance apart all the way across the country. David found himself marveling at his own answers. A new love had been born for both of them.

That Saturday David took Barry on the train to Indianapolis to show his son where he worked. When asked at dinner by Jessica how he had liked the trip, Barry did not have much to say about Indianapolis. However, he talked on through dessert about the train with its changing view, the rattle, the shaking back and forth, and especially how the lights would go out when they entered a tunnel. From that day forward trains were his second favorite – behind Daddy, of course.

That was fifteen long years ago. His first love had been stricken with lung cancer shortly after that day trip on the train. Barry did not quite understand what was happening to his friend as he watched the horrific effects of chemotherapy tear the soul out of this once proud and powerful man. When his father finally succumbed after two years of suffering, the now introverted Barry cried in his room for two days.

After the funeral, Uncle Charlie thought to snatch the pining child off to the Pekesville Depot for an ice cream. While licking his pistachio nut cone, Barry watched the afternoon trains enter and unload. As the few Pekesville residents tottered off each train, Barry noticed that not one of them looked as strong and powerful as his Daddy had. Barry finished his ice cream, a large soda, and four fireballs but refused to leave until the 5:14 arrived and departed.

Now 18 years old, Barry yearned for something different. After his father's death, his mother had to return to teaching. Money was tight so they moved in with Aunt Jane, Jessica's unmarried sister. Under the watchful, overbearing guard of these two overprotective hens, Barry had led what he believed to be a stifled childhood. He had never been allowed to play sports because Jessica thought that the frail, asthmatic child would be hurt. He certainly attained none of his father's physical prowess.

Not much of a student, nor very outgoing, the shy boy was thought rather odd by most of the Pekesville residents. Mostly because he could usually be found sitting on the bench at the Pekesville Station just staring at the trains. Many times his mother had gone to the station and embarrassed him by yelling at him to get home for supper.

Barry had been accepted at the State College at Liston, the next town over. He was scheduled to start in the fall. His mother insisted that he find a summer job to help with tuition. She increased her part-time work at the Pekesville Gazette, the town newspaper, to full-time during each summer to ensure her son's education. However, he did not want to go to college. At least, not yet. He wanted to travel first; to see the country, figure out what he really wanted to do. She would not accept his arguments, and each night the tension mounted.

The following Monday Barry seized his opportunity. His mother informed him that she was taking Aunt Jane to the hospital in Liston for some routine tests. She would not be back until 6:00 p.m.

The man at the newsstand at the Pekesville Depot had become very accustomed to seeing Barry. Many times he had attempted to start a conversation with Barry; getting nothing in return but a vacant stare. That Monday afternoon, noticing the two suitcases at Barry's feet, he tried again, "So, you're finally going someplace?"

Barry nervously laughed, "Yeah."

Jessica and Aunt Jane returned home right on schedule. After quickly searching the house in vain for her son, Jessica circled back to the kitchen where Aunt Jane gasped while reading the note that lay on the kitchen table:

The two women rushed out to the car. They knew exactly where to look. One thought bothered Jessica. Where had he gotten the money for the ticket?

When they arrived at the Pekesville Depot there was a great commotion at the end of track B at the very beginning of the long platform. It had taken a couple of minutes for the train crew to implore the shocked engineer to back off the body it had dragged for over fifty feet until it could stop.

Jessica and Aunt Jane pushed to the edge of the platform. As the train slowly backed up, it revealed two of Jessica's suitcases – both crushed and empty. The silent throng waited with anticipatory horror as the slowly receding engine backed another foot. There, lying in a pool of blood at the foot of the 5:14, was Barry Grant.

For You Bear My Name

By

Faisal Jala

The old city walls that had held invaders at bay for centuries were starting to crumble. As a formidable Republic under powerful patronage, Genoa's gates were a reminder of the true might of the Ligurian town. Built nearly three centuries ago and culminating on St. Andrew's hill, was the grandest of them all – the Porta Sporana. The turrets of the stone walls allowed a panoramic view of the south east part of the fair city. This viewpoint was the child's favorite. He would come here often, escaping the punishment of his father and the disappointment of his mother.

He was now eight years old. He was a curious looking boy, with a slight paunch and bandy legs. What attracted him to others was the intensity of his stare; the look of total concentration on his face. Although he was only eight, he could feel a higher purpose was written for him, he was destined to leave these shores. The churning sea and waves delighted him even as an infant and he often spent his time down in the docks, soaking up all he could - the coarse sailors patois, the smell of the nautical cargo, the spices, the creaking of the aged vessels and the call of the sea.

It was getting dark and the streets were not that safe, so he decided to head home. Due to the increased activity of the ports and trade, you saw a lot of unfamiliar faces, in shape and color, milling about town. Sailors from all over were stopping in Genoa now. The boy found this terribly exciting but his father thought otherwise, he thought it was the beginning of the decline of their society.

As he returned home, he noticed the same scrappy looking Moor waiting in the alleyway next to his home. Again. He had noticed this man three times now, once even on Porta Soprana. The man was clearly a sailor, as he wore the garbs of a seasoned seaman but he also was a light-skinned moor, almost like the sailors from the south coast who were tanned and olive-skilled due to the constant exposure to the sun and the sea.

The boy decided to face the man and ask what he wanted. As he approached him, the man turned into the darkened alley and disappeared. The boy thought about chasing him but at that moment, his younger brother came out to look for him, no doubt sent by his father. The boy decided to not suffer another round of beatings. He quickly entered his home and washed up for supper.

As he entered the kitchen, he noticed his parents arguing about something, as usual. However, lately, they would do something quite curious, they would stop when they noticed he was around. He wondered what that was all about. As he sat on the table, he realized he was really famished and quite forgot about the Moor, until later that night when he dreamt that the Moor was taking him away over the seas to a distant land. The young lad was not scared by this, as he knew it was his destiny to travel afar.

His tutors were all gone. He had spent all morning learning Latin, Castilian and Geography. He particularly enjoyed reading the travels of Marco Polo. He didn't mind studying, it challenged his mind but what he detested was menial work and his apprenticeship at his father's cheese stand really had started lately to cause a rift between his father and the boy. As the eldest, he knew it was expected of him to be dutiful but he knew he could never just follow in his father's footsteps. A lowly mediocre wool weaver and cheese stand owner, Domenico was ambitious but didn't possess the work ethic needed to be a success. He wanted his children to be in wool weaving as well. The boy was determined to make sure that didn't happen.

Returning from the cheese stand one day, he was exhausted. So tired, his usual sharp senses failed to register the scrappy Moor was following him from the cheese stand back to his home. As he neared Via San Donato, the Moor quickened his pace. The boy broke out of his reverie and stopped and turned around. He now faced the Moor. For the first time, the boy noticed the crystal blue pools in the Moor's eyes. He was fixated on them as the Moor spoke.

"You are unhappy with your station in life. Yes?" the Moor said, in halting Spanish. The boy felt compelled to just nod in acquiescence.

"Do you know why?" the Moor asked.

Before waiting for an answer, the Moor put his hand on the boys shoulder and said, "You are destined to not be tied to these shores or any! Listen to me very carefully boy….you are going to have to learn some harsh truths. I was entrusted to tell them to you and then part ways…that is why I am here".

The boy looked up at the Moor and tried to comprehend what all this meant.

He listened intently.

"A long time ago, these shores were not ruled by the Christian man, they were ruled by the righteous descendants of our tribe, the Berbers and the Arabs. We were on a holy mission to expand the teaching of the Prophet but as happens, the evil that men do are often driven by reasons clouded in the past….profit and cruelty overtakes the heart and noble deeds are seldom seen again. We took over this land and all people will remember is the blood spilled by both sides. Soon after, the restlessness of homesick men manifests into marrying into local customs and local women. Many took mistresses but the ones who were noble of thought took wives. One such man was Abbas, my captain and close friend. He had fallen in love with the woman who brought fresh supplies to the boats and they were wedded not long after. She was a wild girl from the hillside village of Monticellu on the island of Corsica."

The Moor paused and let this fact sink in. The boy's expression changed to one of confusion and alarm. His mother was from there too. Was this Moor here on a family vendetta? The boy was now wary of his surroundings and realized he was far from home and tried to devise an exit strategy to San Donato, whose priests would protect him.

The Moor smirked at the boy. He recognized alarm and fear. He was amused.

"No, boy, I am not here to hurt you. We wouldn't be having this lovely chat if that were my intentions. Now, listen carefully, for this will change your life".

The boy stood still. It was late evening and the sun had set. The light breeze was blowing through the streets. He shivered slightly.

"Captain Abbas and this girl were secretly married. Her father, Giacomo, knew not of the affair and the Captain decided it was safer for her to keep this secret. The Captain really loved her and called her his Fontanarossa flower".

The boy couldn't stay silent anymore. He blurted out, "My grandfather is Giacomo from Fontanarossa.

What was this girl's name?" He willed the Moor not to utter the name he knew was his mother's – Susanna.

As if reading this mind, the Moor said, "Though you do not wish it so, it was Susanna".

The Moor watched the boy's reaction to his words, how the dark clouds appeared on his face and a storm was brewing in his mind.

"No, that cannot be. My mother has only been married to my father Domenico. You are telling terrible lies".

"Why would I lie about this? How can I know so much about her? Anyway, I am telling you all this so that you can claim what is yours by rights. Soon after their secret marriage, your mother told Giacomo that she was leaving for she had found work in Genoa. In truth, they were soon to be expecting a child and she needed to hide this from her father. With this excuse, the couple left and sailed away to Genoa and 8 months later, they had a baby boy. Yes, that boy is you".

The boy stood shuddering against the wind. His head was buzzing with all this knowledge. He was very upset with his Mother for hiding this from him but at the same time he was quite excited that his father was a brave sea Captain and not the harsh wool-weaver he had known. He understood the situation but still didn't understand why he was being told this story now. The Moor read this in his countenance.

"You are probably wondering why I am telling you this now?"

Before the boy could acknowledge this, the Moor continued.

"Soon, the tide began to turn for us here in this strange land. We were outcasts and the Vatican's edicts made it difficult for us to remain harmoniously. We lost this peninsula and were driven out. The Captain refused to leave but had no choice as he needed funds to take away your mother and you to his lands. He and I set sail, leaving your mother and you in Genoa when you were still an infant. We set sail for the Canary Islands, as mercenary ships under the banner of Henry the Navigator. There, your father, Captain Abbas, and I, were making much profit from trading spices. Many spoke of mysterious lands out west where much gold was to be found. Your father was now very much desperate to make his fortune quickly and in any way possible so that he could be reunited with his beloved family so he deserted the banner of Henry, which was an offense punishable by walking the plank, and we set sail with a handful of sailors to the uncharted lands. We reached the lands inhabited by the Ciboney and started to look for gold. We noticed the natives wearing small trinkets and jewelry that were pure gold and your father asked the natives to show him where they got it from. They natives explained it was a few days journey and deep into the jungle. It was at this time that your father asked me to return to you and give you this".

The Moor took out a rolled parchment from inside his tattered coat and handed it to the boy. The boy warily took the parchment and unrolled it. It was a cartographers map – but in a language the boy didn't read or understand. The Moor explain, "It's in Arabic. The Arab sailors had been travelling to the western mystery lands hundreds of years ago and they were able to chart their journey. Your father had come into the possession of one of these maps and was able to use it to travel there. He now sent me with these instructions for you – follow the map to his location and reunite as father and son to his next adventure. Untold riches and undiscovered lands lay await for you – but only if you believe this is your destiny. If you think all this is crazy, remain with your cheese stand and your comfortable life here. These were his instructions. Also, make sure you do not discuss any of this with your mother; she needs to be protected from the authorities. She took a major risk in going away once, she needs to be protected now. Do not involve her".

The Moor stopped talking and looked intently at the boy. He thought he would see confusion and cloud the boy's face but instead he saw resolve and the same determined expression he had seen multiple times on the face of his Captain.

"My job is done. I was asked to deliver this to you and to give you the truth. The rest is up to you. I will take my leave".

The Moor took one last long gaze at the boy and turned and walked away.

The boy grasped at the map. He knew what he must do but right now, he needed to get home before his "father" did. He had to start planning how to get on board a ship headed for the mystery lands.

As he walked home, his head was filled with thoughts of riding the oceans with his father, conquering the mystery lands and taking hold of untold riches that lay waiting for him. A semblance of a plan was coming together in his head. He knew what he must do to begin his journey westward towards his destiny and towards his father.

PART 2

It had been nearly a month since the old moor had left him with the map. The boy was restless but also helpless to take action. He was just too damn young to take any action about his future. This debilitating thought paralyzed his mind and he began to despair. He decided he needed assistance from a higher power than his parents to help him escape Genoa – he began to attend daily mass on his route back from the cheese stand. Although he would sit in a church, he prayed to the God of his father to unite them both. Ask and ye shall receive, intoned the priest. So he squeezed his eyes shut and barely breathed while he asked for a way to join his father.

After three weeks of attending mass, he began to question the whole meaning of faith. At first, he was easily distracted by all the ceremony in a mass. He couldn't pray in peace due to the din of the choir, the priest's chanting or the gossip of the churchgoers around him. He began to dislike the whole pageantry of worship and hoped he didn't have to spend much more time trying to find a way out.

Ask and ye shall receive.

He tried to block all sounds around him and focus on his prayers when he couldn't fail to notice the two men talking in loud whispers two rows behind him. They were talking business. The elder of the two was a man known to the boy, he was Don Luis Mendoza, a very prominent trading agent. His "step-" father often sold his wool to him for trade abroad. To falsely emphasize his importance, his "step-" father always bragged to other customers that he was a close business partner of Don Luis, although his father had never had the privilege of meeting the Don but dealt mostly with the younger man sitting next to the Don, who was his clerk Lopez.

Don Luis was very distressed, "This will not do! I need reliable people, not street urchins who will steal my goods and run off!!"

Lopez bowed his head at the rebuke, "I understand, sir, but how was I know this?"

Don Luis hissed, "You recruited them, didn't you? You need to be a better judge of character".

Lopez looked crestfallen. He didn't know what to say.

Don Luis spoke, "Just make sure we get someone to take this journey seriously and deliver the letters, otherwise we are looking at big losses. I need someone who will have a stake in it".

The boy absorbed this conversation and almost immediately, as desperate measures sometimes leads one's mind to come up with novel solutions, his mind began to put a plan together. He would use his "step-" father to send his closer to him real father. It was a balance that pleased the boy.

PART 3

Barely three weeks after that fateful conversation with Don Luis, the boy was making preparations to go on his first sea voyage.

The boy had gone about this plan in a very cunning way. He told his mother that some of his cheese stand customers were talking about the need for reliable apprentices on the trading routes to the Canary Islands. The apprenticeships would not only pay well but also lead to a great future in Don Luis' trading company. They were looking for boys with well-known families. The boy told his mother to speak to her husband to implore Don Luis to take him on.

Things moved very quickly after that. In part, Don Luis needed the shipment to leave for the Canary Islands and so he put aside his reservations for this untested boy.

As the light of the dawn crept into the dark sky, the boy was wide awake, unable to sleep a wink. Although he was excited at the prospect of meeting his real father, he felt grateful to his "step"-father for all he had done, especially during the last few weeks that had enabled him to go on this amazing journey.

The tide was calling. The boat lurched from side to side. The creaks of the planks in the ship, the smell of the salty air and the diving seagulls were all welcome senses for the boy. He soaked it all up and couldn't wait to be a mere speck on the horizon. They set sail around 8 o'clock and the boy heard the navigator yell out, "Toward the south, until sunset: afterwards to the south-west and to the south, quarter south-west". They travelled 15 leagues in this way (60 miles) and this was the way to the Canary Islands.

On his person, he carried the special leather waterproof pouch that carried sealed orders from Don Luis to his agent in the Canary Islands. The boy was told repeatedly to guard it with his life.

The next day, the ship travelled forty leagues and again the navigator bellowed out, "Heading south-west, quarter south".

The boy marveled at the advances that man had made in a few years. His privileged position allowed him to sit in the Captain's cabin and soak in the nautical conversation of the other members of the crew. They argued about politics and naval capabilities. The boy quickly learned that discovery of far-away places were more possible now due to the building of ships such as these called caravels. These were small ships that were able to sail windward more than any other in Europe and evolved from fishing ship designs. Due to this design, they were the first that could leave the coastal cabotage navigation and sail safely on the open Atlantic. This gave the Portuguese and Castilian empires superiority over others in the discovery of lands that could supply the ever-increasing demand for spices such as cinnamon, cassia, cardamom, ginger, pepper, and turmeric. The timing was fortuitous as **the Turks had captured Constantinople in 1453, as a result,** the price of oriental trade goods had gone sky-high in Europe. Only if a route was found to the Indies, a fortune was to be made. Sailors dreamt of a route that bypassed the Muslim-controlled territories of the Middle East and led to China, India and Japan.

The boy learned so much more. He learned a bit more of the ingenuity of his ancestors for they were responsible for the success of navigation into the unknown. With the noticeable presence of Berbers and Moors in their lands, the ship's crew argued at length about the good and bad of having these barbarians in their lands. Some argued that these foreign invaders needed to be kicked out since they were ungodly and not of the church but others argued that the Muslims also believed in the one true God and knew Jesus to be a revered Prophet. There were no clear winners but none could doubt the contribution made to celestial navigation by the Muslim navigators. In fact, fo celestial navigation they all used the Ephemerides, which were astronomical charts plotting the location of the stars over a distinct period of time based on calculations by Muhammad ibn Musa al Khawarizmi, a mathematician and astronomer from the ninth century. His latin name was Algorithmi, the founder of Algebra.

The boy had learned so much already in the 3500 km journey to the Canary Islands. He began to wonder what he would say to his father when he met him. How would be introduce himself? His thoughts helped him pass the time until the sailor in the upper sails called out a land sighting, "*¡Tierra! ¡Tierra!*".

It had been nearly a week since he had left the shores of his home. He quickly realized that the sea would always be his first home. It was in his essence.

As it was quite late, they decided to disembark first thing in the morning. Nighttime was not the safest to unload cargo. The boy waited until the ship was quietly listing in the waves next to the port. He snuck out of his cot and headed towards the other ships that were also berthed in the port. He needed to find one that would be going on the perilous journey that was in his destiny. He looked for the ships that would not be carrying much weight and therefore signaled they were going to bring goods back from the journey and not taking much cargo there. He knew that the ships bound for the new world were carrying just food and supplies but not any goods. He went from ship to ship, peering into the cargo hold, trying to find the right match. After two or three, he found one that looked like the right kind. Also, the crew looked like it was comprised of Moors. The boy decided to put his knowledge of secret shipping routes and manifests of Don Luis ships to good use. He called for the captain of the vessel and implored him to hear his proposal.

The boy spoke bluntly, "Here is my father's map. I need to go to him. Take me to him where the locals call the land Kiskeya. In exchange, I will give you the secret trading papers of Don Luis and the Castilian sea routes. They are worth thousands of Maravedis".

The ship's captain looked at this upstart for a while incredulously. However, he recognized the markings on the map and realized the boy was worth paying attention to since the map bore the mark of Idrisi and the symbol for the Moor trading fleet, which was represented by XMY – symbols whose meaning were long lost. The

Captain was a Moor himself and was very tempted to be privy to the sea routes of the Castilian ships. They set off immediately so that the boy would not have to face the alarm from his boat in the morning when they discover his absence. The Moor caravel slipped out of the dock and headed for the open seas westward.

Travelling ten miles an hour, the sea became rough and the north-east wind commenced to blow, but the captain maintained his route to the west. With varying speeds and covering vast distances, the boy began to wonder if they would ever see land again. He was amazed at how acclimatized the sailors were traveling such endless distances. They traveled for nearly a month covering distances such as sixty leagues and at times, only ten, always at the mercy of the wind and the seas. Food was plentiful as they were stocked very well but the water was rationed. The boy learned to stay out of the sun during the day and this made his thirst more controlled but he loved being out among the stars at night, staring at the galaxy of stars from the sterncastle of the vessel. He quickly learned the art of navigating by ones present position and using the help of the stars, a technique called dead-reckoning. The boy had a natural aptitude for this, though it was very difficult to master. The Atlantic voyage was rarely taken by Europeans at that time, for many believed that the Ocean contained monsters and demons that would destroy your boat. Once the Moors had invaded Spain, there were stories of great Moorish and North African admirals who launched many hundreds of ships towards the unknown lands over the Atlantic but none survived to tell the tale. The most famous of them was the King of Mali Abubakari II, who left his kingdom in the hands of his brother so that he could go exploring. His armada of about two thousand ships left the African coast and some say reached what is now Brazil. Days turned into nights and nights into further long days.

The Secret Game

By

Louise Hart

Just as she had done so many times before, Tanya bounded down the front stairs, stopping only for a moment when she reached the bottom landing in order to listen for movement, voices and other sounds. The house was quiet. All Tanya heard was the hum of the refrigerator running and the tick of the Grandfather's clock that stood at the further end of the hallway just inside the front door. The afternoon sun streaked through the vertical row of windows on either side of the door flooding the hallway with both their light and warmth.

She breathed deeply as though by doing so, she could inhale the sunshine.

Satisfied that she was alone, Tanya turned to the right and walked to the end of the hallway through the dining room and into the kitchen. As she did, Tanya smiled at the sound of her footsteps as her shoes tapped echoes across the polished maple floors. The rhythmic sound seemed to fill the house and gladden Tanya's spirits. The sound keeps the house from feeling empty, Tanya thought with a sense of satisfaction. She found herself almost dancing like Gene Kelly in one of the old movies often aired on television. Tanya's mood lightened as her sense of loneliness and desertion gave way to fascination and satisfaction. She was not alone. There was life in the house and she was that life.

Tanya knew exactly what she was going to do. Her pace quickened as she walked deliberately to the stove that sat at in the inside corner of the kitchen. Once there, she stood quietly for a moment looking out the window at the far end of the kitchen. Light angled in through the window, filling the room with an air of warmth and comfort.

Tanya did not need to look at the kitchen clock to know that it was mid-afternoon, hours after lunch and before supper. She knew this not just from the light, but also, from her stomach. She was not hungry.

As she reached the stove, Tanya stopped and turned around. Tanya had not come to the stove to cook or prepare food, but rather, to start her game.

Tanya had devised her game so long ago, she could not remember the first time that she played it. She just knew that she was good at it and thus, each time that she played it, she changed the rules to make it harder on herself to "win". After all, Tanya had made the game up one day when like today, everyone had left and she was alone. She did not know where the others went then or now, but as she thought about the game, she found herself not caring or wondering where the others were.

Tanya only played the game when she was alone so no one else in her family knew about the game. The game was hers and hers alone. She made it up. She determined the rules. She served as its judge, referee and only player. Because only she ever played the game, she also invariably won the game. Tanya smiled again. She liked the game and being a winner. As winner, Tanya knew she would receive a prize. The prize was not a trophy or a pin to hang on a wall or put on the mantel over the fireplace in the living room. No, Tanya the originator, referee, judge, player and winner of the game did not want a trophy or pin. What she did want was to have her secret wish fulfilled. She made the wish each time she began the game and trusted that this time, like all others, she would find it waiting for her at the end of play.

The basic game was simple. Tanya had to walk from the front of the stove or another spot in the kitchen through the dining room and hallway beyond to the front door without bumping into walls or furniture or tripping over anything. Tanya had not counted how many times she had won her game. Winning was not what it was really all about anyway. She was just pleased that after a few times in which she had faltered and had to start over (one of the game's rules), she had learned to finish the walk without bumping into anything. In time, to make the game more interesting, Tanya began to add more challenging rules to the game. First it was to name where she was, then it was to name what was in the room. Another time, it was to picture what lay beyond the rooms.

One game rule did not change. Tanya had to keep her eyes tightly shut. She did not use a blindfold to keep her eyes closed. She just closed them so tight that she could feel her cheeks puff out beneath them, her nose wrinkle and even her jaw move upwards. As she played the game, her face would relax, but Tanya was proud, she did not open her eyes for then, according to the rules, she would need to start all over.

Today, she decided to use the front of the kitchen stove as her starting line. Thus, as soon as she reached the stove, Tanya turned around, took a deep breath, closed her eyes tightly and stepped confidently forward picturing every element of the room about her in her mind.

Bathroom door to the right, she confidently noted to herself as she felt a flow of air from the open door. She felt so proud of her ability to use her other senses to locate where she was that she was tempted to open her eyes to confirm her adroitness, however, she caught herself. After all, if she opened her eyes, she would have to start all over again and thus it would take longer for her to finish. Besides, she knew that she was right. The bathroom was on her right next to the white archway that divided the kitchen from the dining room. Careful, she cautioned herself. She knew that she must walk in a very straight line and not to veer to the right or left. If she veered to the right, she knew that she would bump into the large dining room set. If she veered to the left, she could walk into the cellar door or the back entranceway. Tanya slowed her pace as she put one foot in front of the other. She concentrated so hard on walking straight that she forgot about the sound of her clicking heels on the wood floor. Instead, she tried to picture the large oak table and eight captain's chairs that she knew was to her right. She had not checked to see if all the chairs were pushed as close as possible to the table. She shook her head slightly as though to chastise herself for missing this detail when she originally walked through the dining room. She made another note to herself to remember to check the position of the chairs in relation to the table the next time before she started the game. Tanya, of course, realized that she need only worry about bumping into or tripping over the end chair for it was closest to the game's course. The other seven chairs did not matter unless she really veered off course which she knew was unlikely. Tanya had played the game enough times to become very good at it.

Still, Tanya took smaller and slower steps as she proceeded through the dining room. Tanya sighed at the sound of her own tense, nervous breathing. She could not look or stop. Looking was against the rules as was stopping. When Tanya first started the game a long time ago, she had instituted no stopping as a rule. Any infraction of the peeking or stopping rule and she would have to start the game all over again. Tanya knew she could cheat and do either or both and no one else would know, but to cheat would take the fun out of the game and deny her the prize she wanted.

Two steps beyond the archway and into the dining room, Tanya decided to veer half a step to her left for she knew that to her left was the open space that led to the back entryway and cellar door. The area was safe. She would not bump into any furniture or walls. The floor too was hardwood and clear so that she would not have to worry about tripping. However, she also knew that if she sidestepped too far, she would bump into the wall and need to back up and move to the right again. That would mean that she would need to start again.

Tanya had proven that she could walk from the kitchen to the front door without opening her eyes many times before so this time, she had decided that she needed to add another new challenge or rule change. She knew that she had to think of something that would challenge her mind. She could change the course layout, she thought, but she liked the challenge presented by the distance she had to "blindly" navigate. Besides, she loved anticipating the warmth of the light at the end of the course. It was like a winner's trophy or reward. She also knew that the front doorway was her ultimate destination, but she did not wish to think of that at the moment.

Most of the previous rule changes had occurred because Tanya feared boredom and wanted to make the game more mentally challenging. Changing the rules seemed to keep the game fresh and challenging for her. This time, she decided that she must picture her surroundings in her mind as she walked the game's course. Tanya had even decided that she must not just picture what the rooms and furniture looked like, but also, be able to "see" the details of each room, each wall, each floor, each ceiling as well as each piece of furniture and to note how and what she felt as she passed each one.

With the change of rules in place, Tanya began the game. She positioned herself in front of the stove, took a deep breath, said ready, set, go, then like an Olympian athlete lunged forward. She was pleased with herself as she pictured the kitchen and exactly where she was in it. She could see the sink and cabinets that lined the outside wall, the nook and benches that surrounded the window at the far end. She pictured the floor tiles and the archways to the other rooms. She smiled tingling with excitement as she recognized the airflow as she passed the open door to the bathroom to the left and the draft from the back entryway and cellar door as she entered the dining room. She felt the coarse brown area rug beneath her feet and "saw" the large cherry dining room table with its eight high backed chairs pushed in close to the table on her right. She challenged herself to remember the exact pattern of her great grandmother's handmade lace doily that she knew decorated its center. She could "see" the large chandelier light that hung above the table even though she knew that it was not on. Except during dinner or when company came, it was seldom on. Because it was not, the small flame shaped lights on the chandelier never burned out. At least, she never remembered their ever having to be changed.

Next she concentrated on the matching antique buffet on the wall next to the table and tried to picture how the room must look with the afternoon light filtered through the cream colored window shades and lace curtains on the far side of the room. She loved how in the muted light made the room feel cozy and homey. In the angled light, no one noticed that the blue green wallpaper was faded or the numerous nicks and scratches on the table and chairs.

Her gate picked up as she congratulated herself, "ah, the game is much more fun today."

She slid slightly to the left so that she could feel the wood floor that extended beyond the rug. She knew that wood floor led to the door sill and that the rug's edge formed a straight line from the corner of the doorway. She thus moved sideways to avoid bumping into the wall as she entered the long entrance hallway. In her mind, she quickly pictured the white wood archway that separated the dining room and hallway. The wallpaper in the hallway was a cream and gold brocade pattern with a large swirled design. As with all the rooms in the house, the high ceiling was white. White was clean and reflected light and thus made the rooms appear brighter than they were. Tanya did not think about that. She was concentrating on the hot air grate that she knew lay ahead of her and the large wooden office desk and chair that she knew was to her left after the staircase. She wondered what the desk might look like if it were not piled high with paper. She was grateful that it was just far enough away from the front door so that no breeze or sudden gust of wind ever blew the papers away. The vision of such a storm of paper made her chuckle as she knew she passed the door to the living room on her right. The door she knew was closed. She touched it as she passed and reached for the front door and windows. She felt the narrow lace curtains on the windows.

She had "won" her game again. Tanya smiled as she allowed herself to open her eyes and look outside. As she did, she saw her "prize". Her mother and siblings were arriving home. Tanya first shouted with glee, then slid down against the doorway, crying. Her mother and older siblings laughed at her tears. Was she afraid? She was not supposed to have awakened while they were gone. How had she gotten herself out of her day bed and dressed? What mischief had she been into? Was she naughty? Was she crying because she was jealous that they had gone shopping without her?

Tanya did not answer. Not yet two years old, she did not have the words to express what she felt or to tell them about her game. She was happy that they were home. It meant she was no longer alone. They never knew of her game even though Tanya never forgot it and would play it for several more years – alone.

When Tanya grew up, she became a teacher and child advocate at an orphanage for young girls. The orphanage served as a home for abandoned, abused and neglected girls. No one ever understood what and how she was able to communicate and help girls who had withdrawn and would not speak to other counselors.

Tanya received many awards for her work, but never told any of her fellow workers the secret that she and the girls shared. Her fellow workers never knew about the game. Tanya was a college graduate. They knew that she had worked her way through college, but so had many of her fellow teachers. Like them, she was from a middle class family. Although Tanya never spoke of her family, the other teachers were certain that Tanya had never had to experience what the girls in her charge did. She would never have graduated from college if she had, they thought.

The other teachers at the orphanage were wrong. Tanya never told them that either. She shared her secret game only with the girls she counseled. She told the girls for she knew that when she did, they would share their secret games with her as well. They shared more, and because they did, Tanya was able to help the girls overcome what had happened to them. The girls became known as Tanya's girls. The girls responded by sometimes calling Tanya mother. Tanya would just smile when they did, just as she would smile when each girl told her about her secret game. As each girl revealed how she came to make up and play her game, Tanya would listen quietly. In her mind, she would play the game with the girl. When the girl finished, Tanya would whisper to her, "Thank you for sharing that secret with me. Your game is special and I could just see you playing your game as you told me of it. I saw you win it. You are a true champion and for that, I applaud you." Tanya would then clap her hands and give the girl a ribbon on a pin as her trophy for winning the game. The little girls eyes always grinned as Tanya pinned the ribbon on their blouse or dress.

After pinning the ribbon on the girl, Tanya would tell her "You know you can play the game whenever you want to in your mind. I had a game that I played when I was your age. Sometimes I still play my game in my mind, but I really like your game. I know you made it up just for when you were alone just as I did. I am so happy that you have told me about your secret game. Now, it belongs to both of us. Now, if you ever decide to play your game again in your mind as I do mine, I hope that you will let me play it with you. That way, you will never play it alone again. I will be watching you and seeing you as you win it again. If you come to me, I will even give you another ribbon."

You are not alone and never will be again. I promise you that."

After she spoke to the girl, Tanya and the girl would just sit silently hugging one another. Tanya loved those moments. Tanya would hold the girl until the girl had to leave. As the girl left, Tanya would reassure her, "You are not alone anymore and while you are here, you never will be again. I promise you that."

Tanya knew that while she was at the orphanage, she, too, would never be alone again either.

Check out more cartoons like this….
www.leftycartoons.com

POETRY

Poetry is an echo, asking a shadow to dance.

~ *Carl Sandburg*

Antique Heirloom

The book lay on the table
Over in the corner
Seldom noticed.

The cover, once a brilliant red,
Now faded to a
Muted crimson.

Its corners, bent and threadbare,
Slightly dingy from
Long ago use.

Some think of it as just a relic
To be packed away
In storage.

But, between its cover
Lies knowledge
Just waiting to be discovered.

The lady sat all alone
Over in the corner
Seldom noticed.

Her eyes, once a vibrant blue,
Now faded to a
Subdued gray.

Her body frail and fragile,
Slightly slumped from
Years of labor.

Some think her usefulness is gone
And they pay her
No attention.

But a wealth of wisdom
Is her gift
To anyone willing to listen.

~ Veronica Free

I Am Not a Pilgrim

I am not a pilgrim.
I am the stillness in the morning dew,
waiting for the sun to set me free.
I am the silence between the music's notes,
waiting for the night to let me be.
I am the presence between my heartbeats,
waiting for my love to come to me.

I am not a pilgrim.
I walk with the wind at my back
on dusty trails through neglected landscapes.

I am the stillness in the morning dew
as the sun heats this deserted land.
I am the silence between the music's notes
as the night wolves begin to band.
I am the presence between my heartbeats
as the fire dies, and I begin to understand.

I am not a pilgrim. I am not a pilgrim
when the wind does not blow across the sand.

    ~ Tom Geddie

My Void

There is a void in my heart
I could never estimate when it had start

It leaves more than the feeling of emptiness
It multiplies the pain of loneliness

Is it possible to be happy?
Yet feel incomplete

The void in my heart
Proves that it is a possibility

I have sat and wondered
How to fill this space?

Can you fill my void?
Which leaves me unwanted and annoyed

I want it to end
Before the pain is shown

But how can you heal it
If the void is unknown

~ Natrissa Baxter

Lead Me

Lead me and I will follow.
I will follow you to the beautiful state of Arkansas to quench
my thirst with natural spring water, tap my toes to the
country, jazz and bluegrass sounds, and hunt for the natural
crystal clear diamonds for you and me to shine in the Delta.
I will follow you to Arkansas where there is a wealth of
natural beauty.

Lead me and I will follow.
I will follow you to the bayou state of Louisiana and listen to
the stories told by the old, educate my children with its rich
history and culture, enjoy the Cajun foods, jazz, gospel, and
zydeco music that fill my soul.
I will follow you to Louisiana where the soil is rich with
plenty of land to plant cotton, rice, sweet potatoes, vegetables,
to raise cattle, to fish and to hunt.
I will follow you to Louisiana to feed my family for a lifetime.

Lead me and I will follow.
I will follow you to the might state of Mississippi to the home
of the blues, where the muddy Mississippi waters flow, where
the culture is richer than the soil, enjoy gospel, catfish and
hushpuppies.

Lead me and I will follow you around the Delta.

~ Linda Mays-Logan

THE SCRABBLE ADDICT

Check out more cartoons like this….
www.inkygirl.com

Life is but an illusion

Every day he looks into the mirror; mislead to believe
who he sees
In the mirror are he, not realizing his soul is his
companion and his
Flesh subjected to decay, I see a young man troubled, lost
in
His own illusions, seeking foolish pleasures as his refuge
of his attachments and desires
Which he believes will bring him happiness beyond his
wildest
Dreams.
But the true path he seeks is within thee, that which is not
an illusion but reality
He is an entity, a soul, a force strongly connected as one
with the universe, but until one realizes these elements of
truth
Only then will he be truly free

~ Giovanni Sticco

Listen Up

Listen up
What do you know about peace?
This means stop the fighting
The foolishness needs to cease

Listen up
There's too much terror
Something is wrong
We need to correct the error

A solution
We definetly need
It's getting out of hand
Killing is a greed

War
This goes on day after day
Hatred all around us
There has to be a better way

The terrible stuff that we do to each other
The bad news that I watch or read
Something has to change
Love has to lead

Let love in
Let love guide you
Don't wait
Just do

It's up to you
It's up to me
We have the power
We can stop the insanity

Less fight
Love more
I represent peace
This is what I stand for

~ Jason O' Neal Williams

God Loves You More Than I Do

I love you very much,
I'll do anything for you.
But God loves you more
Than I do.

I love you with all I have,
And all I'll ever be.
God loved you with his son,
Who died upon a tree.

I love you, I always will,
More than I can tell.
God loves you with Heaven
And life eternal

~ Penny Reyes

You Are Remembered

You are remembered
I remember everything
It's just now you're gone
Everything changed

You are remembered
From your smiles, kisses and hugs
You are remembered
From showing all the love

You are remembered
From down to up
You are remembered
From wishing good luck

Don't worry
I know you use to get mad and catch a bad
temper
But you are still remembered

I will always love you
Through January through December
And you will always be remembered

~ Faith Willis

My Lover

My lover's eyes are deeper than the sea
His head is crowned with wisdom of his years
His lips speak words which flow with life to me
And in his arms am I secure from fears
What day found me in danger or distress
That hero did not dash to set me free?
What day did I not lift my voice to bless
The name of God for sending him to me?
Our children blessed with tender, loving touch
With gentle admonition he will nourish
For each plant in his garden cares as much
They prosper and succeed, he sees them flourish
A man of vision, power, strength, and prayer
By heaven's grace I have this life to share.

~ Phyllis Walker

The Darkness

The darkness lurks among the shadows
In every corner of my mind

It feeds on every insecurity
And weakness that it finds

When I try to fight or resist it
It claws long valleys across my soul

No, I can't deny its existence
Because I can feel it staring holes

The darkness is cold and empty
So lonely I can't describe

It haunts me when I close my eyes
And terrorizes me at night

When I'm stumbling and shaky
The darkness squeezes me tight

If you listen you'll hear it stalk me
Even our heart beats are synchronized

Wakes me in a sweat when I'm dreaming
It finds me where ever I hide

The darkness is part of the madness
It's the madness that I understand

No, there's no use in me pretending
It consumes me whenever it can

~ Patricia Baker

Old Soul

I have succumbed to death many times.
It is the memories of these past lives that keep me alive.

I am no exception to falling to death.
I am no healer of the faith as I hear their whispers
under their breath.

My soul is very old, yet willing to live in many human
shells.
It beats being a saint in heaven and burning in
everlasting hell.

I die and then I live again.
Don't worry about me as you will always remain my
friend.

If you could do what I do then maybe we will see each
other again.
Many friendships in this life, the past, and the next, it
won't end.

So for now I say goodbye to you in this life we live.
Maybe I will see you in the next life we give.

~ Edward Bortot

Night's Wish

Once I dreamt a dream,

And dreamt of angels over black seas,

Spreading wonderfully their frozen wings,

Looking for the perfect pearl,

Amidst thousands of nameless pearls,

Revealing to me the night's wish:

Present & Future, one single time for me!

I dreamt of musical pearls and scores,

Long scores played,

And waters from the tears' flood,

Bringing me to you, giving you my blood,

Swimming with the mermaids,

Writing poems on love with love,

Uniting two planes that cannot unite:

Pearls of time in mermaids' realm,

And flying angels defying reality instead…

Once I had a dream,

Once I dreamt this dream,

I dreamt of writing lines in red,

Of having had a dreamt dream,

A dream of mine, of love & lust,

Of wishes in the eternity,

And this could be it:

In love forever you & me.

~ Hector J. Fuentes

Returning Home

The disused road down,
My distance memory of
An Irish childhood,
Played the waves their
Haunting sounds for a
Prodigal son's return,
From the American land
Of a second chance for
Hopes and dreams of this
Irish soul.

Down the cove the Irish
Mist creeps over the hills,
swirling white silence.
The land welcomes me
Home the falling rain,
Baptism of an Irish Mother,
For her lost son.

I walk the broken path,
Weeds cover the childhood
Memories of a past,
Forgotten with an American
Twang and a New York attitude.

Roll back the hills with
Memories of previous,
Steps alongside my Mother,
The Father's boat with
Hand line caught fish,
Cries of the seagulls invoke
Summertime moments.

I turn up the lapels of
My winter coat glance to
The kissed skies of Mother's
Tears knowing I'll never return,
From my past the same again.

~ Robin McNamara

Irish Toasts

Three Great Things in Life

There are three great things in life
And they will take away any strife
The first is a woman's love
For on this list, there is nothing above
The second are great friends
For whom with you will never have to make amends
The third is good beer or whisky in a glass
Served to you by a pretty Irish lass

~ Marcus Blake

Here's to all the kisses I've had
From many, many, many an Irish lad
Some were short, some were tall
But I have loved them all
So if you'd like, you can kiss this Irish lass
Just make sure to have me home for mass

~ Mary Waters

When you find good whiskey or beer
That is how the lord will bless you
And you will be filled with so much cheer
That even the devil can't help but pray for you.

~ George Clark

To all the days here and after
May they be the end of bad times
And filled with everlasting laughter
So that your joy will carry over many lifetimes

~ The Drunken Irish Poet

May you find your way
With Good Whiskey and Beer
On this St. Patrick's Day
And always be full of good cheer

~ The Drunken Irish Poet

Gather Old Friends

Gather ye old friends to this hallowed place.
Where the Guinness is smooth like satin and lace
It is time to leave your worries at the door.
And drink, and sing, and dance upon the floor.
Where else would we be on this perfect night
But only a place that serves whiskey and Guinness right.
For in this great pub there is no better place to be at
Especially the seat next to mine where this Irish lass sat.
And if I be the luckiest man tonight
That which shines upon her will be the morning light.

~ Marcus Blake

(C) 2018 R STEVENS ::: DIESELSWEETIES.COM

Check out more of these comics at…
www.dieselsweeties.com

HAIKU
Themes

March 2019 Theme

"Words"

Spring, a word for hope
Where all things are possible
And we start over

~ Marcus Blake

Some buy you diamonds.
I offer something solid:
I give you my word.

~ Ryan Miller

Scenic Exhibits
Very few words can describe
These perfect moments

~ Anonynmous

Simple things to say
But words can be powerful
When spoken with heart

~ Anonynmous

One Act Plays

From this Moment From Now On

By

David Thomas

Setting and Characters

We have a man and woman in their mid-forties. Both talk as if alone unless otherwise noted. All stage settings and most character movements are left to the discretion of the director.

Woman: There he was on top of me.

Man: We were having sex.

Woman: Grunting and sweating.

(pause)

Grunting.

Man: And then she said…

(pause)

she said…

Woman: I don't know what it was about that moment…

Man: She said it!

Woman: With him laying on me still…

(pause)

spent, breathing hard in my ear…

(pause)

I said it.

Man: She said she loved me.

Woman: I told him that I thought…

(*pause*)

I thought that just maybe I was falling in love with him.

(*silence*)

Man: I told her she was being stupid.

(*pause*)

She didn't even know who she was talking to.

Woman: He put his finger to my lips to quiet me.

(*silence*)

I kissed his finger. He kissed my forehead. He was so soft and gentle.

(*pause*)

So like a virgin; shaking like a leaf kissing me.

(*pause*)

(*softly*)Kissing me.

(*pause*)

No wonder I was falling in love.

Man: How could she say she loved me?

Woman: *(softly)* No wonder.

Man: How could she possibly mean it?

(silence then turning to woman suddenly, almost violently)

How?!

Woman: *(facing man and talking calmly to him)* What was that?

Man: How could you say you were falling in love?

Woman: Easy; I thought I was.

Man: Well damn it…

(slight pause)

What do you mean "thought"?

Woman: Never mind.

(crosses to man and starts rubbing his shoulders)

You're too tense.

(pause)

You think too much.

Man: *(pulling away, no longer speaking to woman)* Such soft thoughts, such strange words.

(pause)

I think I told her that. *(to woman)* Didn't I tell you that?

Woman: Tell me what?

Man: That you think too much.

Woman: You may have now that you mention it.

Man: I could've said you don't think enough.

Woman: Are you sure?

(pause)

Maybe that was another woman you were laying atop arguing with.

(pause)

I know me and I don't think it was me who didn't think enough.

(pause)

No. I'm sure of it. That was another woman.

Man: I was right you know.

Woman: How's that?

Man: You think too much.

Woman: *(no longer speaking to man)* I think too much? Well maybe I do. So what? I mean, what of it?

(pause)

So much made from such a simple thing said in that post-coital glow.

Man: What could she have been thinking?

(pause)

That's the problem with women who think too much, you never know what the hell they're thinking.

(*pause*)

Not really.

(*pause*)

Hardly ever.

Woman: Men.

(*pause*)

They can make the biggest deal out of nothing.

(*pause*)

Not that saying "I love you" is nothing.

(*pause*)

I just didn't mean anything by it.

(*pause*)

Not at the time.

Man: *(turning to woman)* We changed after that, didn't we?

Woman: No.

(pause)

You changed.

Man: Oh bull; you went around looking me all cow eyed.

(pause)

Hopeless.

Woman: I had always looked at you "cow eyed" as you so sweetly put it.

(pause)

We looked at each other that way.

(pause)

You're the one who stopped.

Man: Are you sure? Maybe that was another man.

Woman: Maybe.

Man: *(turning away from woman)* I didn't know what to do then.

(pause)

How to act toward her.

Woman: He was so cute.

(pause)

It was funny how he ran around trying to convince me I didn't mean what I'd said.

Man: I didn't love her then.

(pause)

I fought her.

(pause)

I fought the idea. How could I love her?

(pause)

I didn't even know how she could say it.

(pause)

And when she did no less!

(pause)

Right after sex and all.

(pause)

I was lousy in bed. So nervous.

(pause)

I don't even know what I was nervous about. She hadn't even said it yet.

(pause)

But still; there I was like a scared puppy.

(pause)

And she said she loved that?

Woman: He tried so hard to deny it all.

(pause)

I honestly think he thought he didn't love me.

Man: *(to woman)* I didn't love you.

Woman: You didn't?

Man: No.

(pause)

I don't think so.

(pause)

I don't know. I might have.

Woman: So you didn't love me?

(pause)

That's what you're telling me?

Man: No. No; I didn't love you.

(pause)

That's what I'm telling you.

Woman: Yes you did.

Man: Don't tell me what I thought.

Woman: Then you're saying to me now that you don't love me?

Man: That is indeed what I am saying.

(silence)

Woman: Do you love me now?

(no answer from man)

Do you love me now?

Man: I'm thinking!

Woman: Do you need to?

(no answer)

You think too much.

Man: No, that's you.

Woman: Don't evade the question.

(pause)

Do-you-love-me?

Man: I told you I was thinking about it.

Woman: Time's up.

Man: God I hope not.

(man moves to stand in front of woman placing his hands on her face and kissing her softly)

Woman: I told you not to evade the question.

Man: What was it you asked?

Woman: Do-you-love-me-now?

Man: I guess so.

(pause)

Yes.

Woman: Yes?

Man: Yes.

(pause)

After ten years of marriage, I still love you.

(silence, they embrace and kiss, fade lights)

~ END ~

For Producers: *If you would like to produce this play, then please contact the writer at…*

David Thomas
214-515-8311
draythomas@gmail.com

Check out more cartoons like this….
www.leftycartoons.com

Articles *and* Editorials

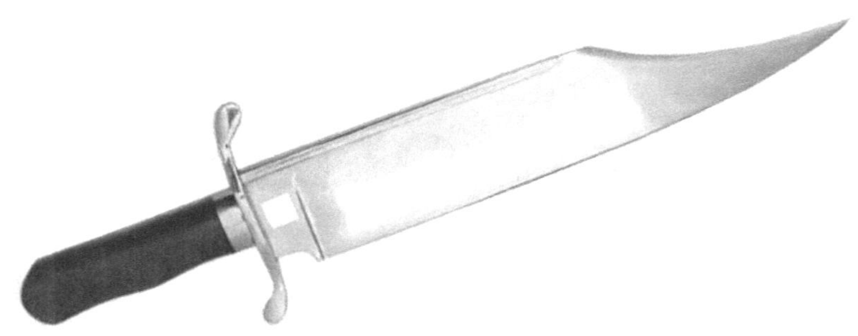

Bowie Knife:

The Symbol of Southern Masculinity

By
K. Scott Cooper

History is full of symbols. Symbols have power because they give us greater understanding and greater context. A symbol can be anything from an inanimate object, an object or animal in nature, or can even be a human being. Southern culture in the 1800's was very reliant upon symbolism in their ideology. One such prominent symbol of southern culture is the Bowie knife. A knife so inundated in its own mythology and folklore that it brought about an almost deification of Jim Bowie. This deification would be used as one of the many examples that would aid in the building of the platform southern leaders utilized to condone the civil war. It became a contributor and one of the many facets for what made a man "a man" in southern society. This symbolism illuminates the state of mind and naivety directed to the romanticism of the civil war, this romanticism would leave confederate soldiers mentally unprepared for the horrors of war that they would face.

These Ideologies would be the cornerstones and groundworks for motivations that southern statesmen and southern plantation owners would use to defend the southern way of life. It also speaks to a level of arrogance and imagined superiority. Before we can dive into what created this mindset and the platform that it used to build and how it grasped upon this symbolic image of the bowie knife, we must first understand what made this knife popular and what lead to its innovation and invention. It all begins with Jim bowie and the actions that began the incident on September 19th 1827 known as the Videlia Sandbar Fight.

The sandbar on which the famous fight takes place and for which it was named, is a long, heavily wooded peninsula on the western shore of the Mississippi river, in Natchez Mississippi. An area long used for settling disputes in the form of duels, facilitated for use as the arena for such disputes as early as 1806 by the owner of the connecting plantation Joseph Videl, owner of the early French plantation Concordia.[1]

The peninsula has one way in and one way out which makes it ideal for duels. Despite it being heavily wooded, the center is bare, sandy ground cluttered with driftwood, which could be easily cleared away and piled aside for the duels that were so commonly occurring there.[2] The initial issue that brought Jim Bowie to this place was for a duel of which he himself was a not part, but rather served as one of the numerous seconds for the arguing parties. The initial argument began between Dr. Thomas Maddox and Samuel Levi Wells who agreed to duel to satisfy aggression and aggravations caused by the circulation of rumors and gossip

---

[1] Thorp pg. 9
[2] Thorp pg. 9

regarding General Montfort Wells that was the older brother of Samuel.[3]

Samuel agreed to participate in the duel on behalf of his brother due to his brother's much older age and exceptionally poor eyesight brought about by severe cataracts. Each man formed a party of seconds to ensure the fairness of the fight, and ensure the satisfaction of the results of the duel, as well as to serve as witnesses. Wells' seconds numbered five, being George C. McWerthers, Thomas Jefferson Wells (another brother of Samuel and Montfort), General Samuel Cuny and his doctor of a brother (This man's name was not mentioned in any account, simply named as "Doctor Cuny"), and Jim Bowie. The Maddox party consisted of Major Norris Wright, Colonel Rodger H. Crain, and the brothers Alfred, Carey, and Denny Blanchard, Denny himself being a doctor, as is custom for both parties to include a physician in their attendance[4].

While it is known that the main point of the duel was to sate the discourse brought on by the spreading of rumors, each man in the party of both sides, however had grounds and reason to bare grievances against the other party's members, such as the known and public dislike between Bowie and Wright. Wright, served as a bank director and had previously been a party to denying Bowie a bank loan after Bowie had indorsed Wrights political opponent in a sheriff's election. Wright had fired a pistol round at Bowie in the streets of Alexandria. The round missed Bowie, but it was a close miss as the round grazed his ribcage, and Bowie then attempted an advance at Wright before the two were separated to prevent the furthering of violence in the streets.

The Duel between Maddox and Wells would begin as the sun light of the day settled on the heights of Natchez, and would turn out to be a quick and bloodless one. Both met with pistols at ten paces, fired at each other, reloaded and fired again. Both volleys missed the intended targets, after which both men met in the middle and agreed that honor had been met by both sides. The

---

events that unfolded after are the source of American legend for years to come and had numerous bodies of witnesses claiming to have been at the scene, but no historical evidence supports additional eyewitnesses other than those already present. As the two parties drew closer to one other following the duel General Samuel Cuny called out to Colonel Robert H. Crain "We might as well settle our troubles, here and now."[5] In the same instance Cuny reached to draw his pistol. Crain being an experienced duelist, and holding the reputation for dueling to settle debts that he owed rather than paying them as it was easier to settle, had his pistol already in hand and fired first.[6] The round was meant for Cuny, but Bowie stepped in front of Cuny taking the ball to the hip and knocking him to the ground. Cuny fired his pistol the moment he completed his draw, doing so as Bowie fell to the ground.

Cuny struck Crain in the pistol arm, however, Crain remained standing and with his uninjured arm draw a second pistol and fired at Cuny. Crain's second pistol round struck Cuny in the left side of his chest, knocking him to the ground and fatally wounding him. As Bowie lay prone, Major Norris Wright fired at Bowie and missed, upon which he discarded his pistol and drew his sword cane to advance upon Bowie. As Bowie rose to face his attackers he drew what would be described as a "Butchers Knife" and advanced to face Crain who was the closer of the two attackers.

Crain, prepared for Bowie's advance, repelled the advance by striking Bowie in the head with the butt of his empty pistol. The blow dropped Bowie to his knees and provided Wright with the exact moment he was looking for, while also being the moment needed for Crain to retreat. As Bowie remained stunned on his knees from Crain's strike, Wright advanced and lunged forward with the long thin stiletto style blade of his sword cane and ran Bowie through the chest. The blade protruded several inches out of the back of Bowie, then Wright attempted to retrieve the blade by placing his foot on Bowie's chest and leveraging out the blade.

---

[5] Thorp pg. 14
[6] Thorp pg. 12

The next few seconds was seen as a blur by the few onlookers, as the thin blade of the sword cane snapped when Wright attempted to free it from Bowie's chest. It was also in that moment that Bowie grabbed Wright by the wrist holding the remainder of the sword cane and threw him to the ground as he struck Wright with his knife, disemboweling and killing Wright. As Bowie rose to his feet he attempted to remove the broken protruding blade from his chest and in doing so made himself an easy target for the shot fired by Alfred Blanchard some twenty feet away.

Alfred Blanchard's ball struck Bowie in the left arm, but Bowie shrugged off the injury as he rushed Blanchard with the knife and attacked him. Bowie stripped the flesh from Alfred Blanchards forearm with a single strike, Blanchard then retreated in the direction of his brother Carey to avoid further engagement of Bowie. Carey Blanchard fired a pistol shot at Bowie as his brother escaped, but the round missed Bowie all together, but bought Alfred enough time to escape Bowie's range. As Carey Blanchard turned to escape with his brother Alfred and the rest of the Maddox party, he was shot and wounded by George McWherters.

Bowie then turned to his party and collapse seconds later from his immense injuries and significant loss of blood. He was immediately set upon by Dr. Cuny, who before was vainly attempting to intervene on the behalf of his previously mortally wounded brother. Dr. Cuny removed the protruding sword blade, both pistol balls, and managed to staunch the bleeding, ultimately saving Bowies life.[7]

The knife Bowie used to inflict this kind of carnage upon his opponents was as before described "a Butcher's Knife" and has even been referenced to later in newspaper articles retelling the event, as a "Butching Knife." However, the description between these two knives only differs in the word alone, their descriptions are the same and both are ultimately an interchangeable preferential term for the same item. Irregardless of these descriptors for the knife that Bowie used during this event, it was

---

[7] Thorp pg. 15

not the knife that would become the famed Bowie knife. Based off of averages, the description of the bowie knife owned by John Palette mentioned in Raymond W. Thorp's work *Bowie Knife,* (1925):

"In 1853 I lived on a plantation near Port Gibson, Mississippi. At that time, most men wore knives and pistols as commonly as we wear hats. Bowie-knives were not uncommon, and I owned one in which I took a especial pride. This knife came to me through a horse trade with a man named Emory, who had been an overseer cn the Buzzard Plantation in western Arkansas. When I received the knife I was told that it was made by an Arkansas blacksmith "who made the best blades in the world." I do not recall his name, but I can describe the knife. The blade was fourteen inches long, single-edged to the curve of the point, where both sides had been keened to a razor-edge. The curve started about two and one-half inches from the point. On the back or rib of the blade there was a fighting guard of hardened brass. It was covered with nicks, showing that Emory or a former owner had engaged in fights with the weapon. The back piece was used in parrying blows.

Hardened brass is a much softer metal that hardened steel, and the parrying guard was made of the softer metal in order to catch and hold a blow, otherwise the blade would slide and cut the holder, who naturally would be on the defensive. Whenever you see a knife with a strip along the back of the blade, you may be sure that the weapon was made for killing men, and not beasts of the field.

This hilt of this knife was protected by a two-pronged crossguard, the overall length of the latter being about three inches. Others I have seen were even longer. The blade was one and seven-eighths inches wide at the guard, and the heel or rib of the blade was three-eighths inch in breadth. The handle of this blade was made of seasoned black walnut, and was made in one piece into which the shank of the blade had been sunk, the latter being pawled or nobbed at its end."[89]

In addition to the multiple descriptions given of Jim Bowie's knife, there are some confusions of the variations of the bowie knife, and often get confused with similar yet different types of blades, such as that of the Arkansas Toothpick, which is also described by Palette in Thorp's work:

"I knew a knife-fighter from Mississippi who used an Arkansas Toothpick. It had a sixteen-inch blade, double-edge, and tapered to a 'toothpick' point. He used it as a throwing knife; said he had killed two men with it. [sixteen inches was nothing remarkable; an English "official report" describes a knife "manufactured by Bunting and Son, of Sheffield, the blade of which was eighteen inches long, ornated in beautiful

---

[8] Thorp pg. 30-31
[9] Fig.1 for comparative example

tracery, and worded 'The Genuine Arkansas Toothpick.'" And a twenty-three-inch blade will appear later herein.]"[10][11]

It's easy to see how an outsider might misconstrued these knives as being the same, fundamentally lacking the ability to discern the two, and to speak in plain terms: A Big knife is a Big Knife.

At that time, the Bowie knife had yet to have been created. Many have attempted to take credit for the crafting of the Bowie knife, the origins of which have seemed to have unparalleled mystique as if it were Excalibur given by the lady of the lake. The legendariness behind who invented this knife gives it almost a mythical quality, one that could be easily manipulated and coupled with the southern heritage ideology that the southern states and its people are direct descendants of the knights of old, and simply an American extension of a much greater and glorious heritage of history of rule. Two examples of individuals who claimed or were given credit to have made the knife are Jim Bowie's Brother, Rezin P. Bowie (who is favored and credited by several encyclopedia and dictionary sources) Another being Captain Reese Fitzpatrick, who was favored for creating the bowie knife for his extensive superior work during the bowie knife's most popular time in comparison to US made bowie knives at the time,- (which will be discussed shortly), Crafted the first bowie bayonets, and for the forging of special presentation blades presented to military heroes.[12]

It's been through my research that one such name that is already among the names listed and accredited to making the bowie knife, and based on my findings whom I believe to be the actual creator of the bowie knife, James Black. Black's own history supports the concept of him being the knifes creator through his well-known prowess of knife making, which led to Bowie seeking him out in order to make the blade. Keeping in mind that at this current period of time, no pattern blade yet existed called the "Bowie Knife." In order to understand what drew an experienced

---

[10] Thorp pg. 32

[11] Fig.3 for comparative example

[12] Thorp pg. 89

knife fighter like Jim Bowie to commission a blade from Black, was that Black had already made a name for himself among the knife fighting community for fabricating and creating a style of knife that's express intent and purpose was specifically for knife fighting.[13] As I will now go on to explain, the misfortune experienced by Black after he fabricated what would become the Bowie Knife, removed him from the crafting field and paved the way for other individuals to claim credit for the creation.

James Black was born in Hackensack, New Jersey May 1st 1800. At the age of four, his mother passed, and his father promptly remarried. At the age of eight, due to his dislike of his step mother and conflict with his father for marrying her, he ran away from home to Philadelphia. Shortly after his arrival, he was discovered by local authorities to be a runaway; yet due to not wanting to be returned, refused to disclose from whence he came.[14] Black's physical size was large for his age, and had a strong physique, due to this and his not knowing his own age, he was believed to be older (about eleven), and as such was standard custom of the time this led to him being placed in an apprenticeship of a silversmith. He excelled and became a finished crafter, and worked the craft until 1818, upon which time, they believed him to be 21, and therefore old enough to embark on his own, and was released from the service of the Silversmith. He was in reality, however, only 18 years old. Black did not have the ability to establish his own trade due to the surplus of already employed silversmiths in the surrounding areas, which led him to having to take odd-jobs over the years. During one of these odd-jobs as a deckhand on a steamer engine, he made the companionship of a young man named Elijah Stuart. Stuart and Black would later end up in a settlement known as Washington Hempstead County, Arkansas in the spring of 1824. Stuart went on to build a Tavern, and Black went on to find employment under a local blacksmith by the name of Shaw.[15][16]

---

[13] Thorp pg. 22,30
[14] Thorp pg. 18
[15] Thorp pg. 19
[16] Fig.5 photo featuring James Black

Black having no money to invest in Shaw's smithing business, reached an agreement with the forge master that Shaw and his two sons would do all the rough work such as shoeing horses, making wagon rims, and making supplies for settlers traveling to Texas, and Black was to focus on making and mending guns and knives for the travelers and frontiersmen. This arrangement would prove extremely beneficial to both Black and Shaw and it was only a short time before Black was made an equal partner of the shop. All was well and good, until Black fell in love with Shaw's Eldest Daughter, Anne. Because of custom and laws of the time, Black and Anne were not able to marry because of Shaw's Disapproval. The reason for this forbiddance was never explained, and relations between Shaw and Black deteriorated swiftly.[17] Black had a very strong moral compass, which led him to decide to leave to spare Anne any discomfort, and headed for the frontier to try to make his way by selling his equal partnership back to Shaw. When his prospects on the frontier were brought to a sudden and abrupt end due to circumstances outside of his control, he was forced to return, during which time he attempted to retrieve some of the money that Shaw was meant to return to him for the partnership.[18] Much to Black's surprise and dismay, the way the contract drawn up by Shaw had been worded, the agreement stated that Black had signed away his partnership, without any compensation. Due to his hurry to leave, he had signed without realizing this knowledge of the conditions.[19] In that moment, Black decided to retaliate, by marrying Anne without Shaw's permission, and once the couple began living together, Black set up a rival Blacksmithing operation.

Blacks business would become extremely successful and it would not be before long that Black found himself smithing day and night to keep up with the demand of clients. Demand and work grew so much for black's operation that he took on help from one of his brothers-in-law for help at the shop. Despite the

---

17 Thorp pg. 19-20
18 Thorp pg. 20
19 Thorp pg. 20

closeness of Black and his coworker, Black never shared with him the process of the hardening and tempering methods Black used on his blades.

Tempering is a process of heat treating by which the "toughness" (or what gives the steel its strength,) of the material is increased. This is in part to two main based components of steel Iron and carbon in the form of carbide crystals. These carbide crystals and the amount of which within the steel determines a blade's ability to maintain hardness and hold an edge. This is achieved by heating the blade to a particular temperature based on the quality of the steel. When heated to the proper temperature the carbides start to melt and dissolve within the iron matrix in which they are held, which is created during one of the many previous steps taken before tempering. Once the steel reaches this stage, it is ready for a step known as quenching. Quenching is the term used for the rapid cooling of the heated steel by placing it into water or oil to change the rigidity and tensile strength of the steel by the sudden temperature change on the molecular level. This process creates needlelike structures inside the carbide crystals. When this occurs, the steel has reached its maximum level of hardness. Its internal components at this point, is under immense strain making the steel extremely brittle. In this state, the steel could hold the sharpest of an edge, but runs the high risk of shattering if struck, defeating the purpose of the blade. In order to bring the blade to a workable state, to where it will be able to function as it is intended, it must be evenly heated throughout the entire length of the blade. This is determined by a visual color change in the heated material which is often referred to as a "dull red"[20]

Black was so guarded and secretive of his signature method of tempering that he performed his processes alone in the shop hidden away by a drawn curtain, hung at the back of his shop.[21] His forbade any access of anyone, including his wife past the point of the curtained corner of his shop. His need for secrecy was only matched by his standard of quality he held his work to, Black

---

[20] Hrisoulas pg. 55
[21] Thorp pg. 21

would test his blades with something he referred to as the "Hickory Test".

After the finished edge of the blade was complete, Black would work a seasoned hickory block with the newly finished edge for the time of an hour. Black did this as a method of preforming an extreme stress test on the blades ability to hold an edge, if blade dulled after that hour it would indicate a failure in the hardening or tempering process or would identify material component issues in the metal used to forge the blade.[22][23] After the hour Black would take the tested blade and attempt to shave the hairs from his arm. If the edge did not meet Blacks standards by smoothly and cleanly removing the hairs from his arm the blade would be deemed a failure and discarded. This was just one of Black's twelve processes he felt no need to hide from the curious minds that sought to learn his methods. Black's skill as a cutler would draw attention from far and wide, and as far as St. Louis and New Orleans, and it wouldn't be long before Black's name would reach the ears of Jim Bowie.

Jim Bowie arrived in Black's shop December 1830, and with him he carried a widdled wooden form shaped like the blade he wished Black to forge for him. This is where it could be easily misconstrued as to Rezin Bowie, Jim Bowie's aforementioned brother, being the creator of the Bowie knife, since he was the one who designed the wooden form and widdled the block which would be the blueprint for the blade commissioned to be made by Black. Black agreed on the design and instructed Bowie to return in four weeks' time, upon Bowie's return Black presented the blade Bowie had designed and presented him with a similar knife the Black himself had designed.[24] This was outside the normal standard of operation for Black's shop, were as before Black preformed his work to the letter of specification the client ordered. But in this case Black felt compelled that he should make a second blade as he thought the knife should be made. Bowie tested each knife for the desired qualities of his preferences and decided to take

---

[22] Thorp pg. 21
[23] Hrisoulas pg. 95
[24] Thorp pg. 22

the blade of Black's design. Almost immediately after Jim Bowie
left Black's shop, he was set upon by three men who were hired by
John Sturdivant to kill him.[25] The three men rushed Bowie from
concealed cover of nearby underbrush, brandishing knives. One
grabbed ahold of the bridal of Bowie's horse upon which, Bowie
drew his new weapon whilst leaning forward, and lopped the
man's head cleanly off. One of the other bandits swiped at Bowie,
glancing his calf. Injured, Bowie leapt from the saddle, and
advanced towards the man that struck him, slashing across the
man's stomach, disemboweling him. The third man, witnessing the
horror, attempted to flee the scene, but Bowie caught him and as it
was described, split his skull down to his shoulders.[26] Stories of this
event caught on and became popular culture of the time, and
innovated the desire for everyone to own a "Bowie Knife."

The popularity of the knife spread so far and so much that
there were schools dedicated to skilled knife fighting established in
major cities such as St. Louis, Chicago, New Orleans, and the like.[27]
Popularity of the knife reached an international level when a
design of Bowie Knife started being mass-produced and sold back
to Americans coming from Sheffield England. The selling of bowie
knives was so widespread that practically everyone had one, from
the lowest of poor farmers, to the upper most members of high
society.[28]

This incident created the legend of the "Bowie Knife" that
Black would go on to produce in the hundreds.[29] Black's luck
would starkly change in the summer of 1839, a year after his wife's
death, illness and a clubbing by his rival and father-in-law left
Black almost completely blind. Black's life would worsen greatly in
a short time, in which Black was completely blind, homeless, and
destitute.[30] It is by the kindness of others that take in Black and care

---

[25] Thorp pg. 23, see footnote three. Chapter 13 pg. 128-131
[26] Thorp pg. 23
[27] Thorp pg. 36
[28] Thorp pg. 45-46
[29] Thorp pg. 29-30
[30] Thorp pg. 24-25

for him until his death in 1872, Black never spoke of his techniques to anyone else until May 1st 1870 were Black attempted to finally share the information he had kept secret for so long, only to discover in his own horror to have forgotten completely.[31]

It can be seen how easy it would be for someone to take credit or to claim fabrication for the creation of the Bowie knife after Black's hardships in 1839, seeing as he almost virtually disappeared, was completely removed from the crafting scene whatsoever, and had everything either destroyed or taken away from him by the malevolence of his father in law. However, it is not Black dropping off the face of the earth that gives the Bowie knife its mystique, it only heightens the legend.

This is where the Bowie will take a symbolic turn; This is the beginnings of where the cultural ideals of being rough and tumble well before the "innovation", and as shown before in the description of Jim Bowie's Sandbar duel, that duels where already occurring and already popular. Whereas most of Europe has discarded the idea of the duels, it was still very much alive and well in the South. The reason for that being how the dynamic of our country worked at the time. For he most part, the south was producing goods and shipping them to the North. That was the upper south, where you'd see the majority of cotton plantations and most of the slavery, while the rest of the south was rather rural and backwoods, white communities. In these communities the sense of the frontier and the feel of struggle was very real. It's here that you see that all of their transactions, all of their economic decisions based on crops, cattle, and the like is based off of their survival and ability to feed and protect their families.[32] There is a sort of cast system where there is honor within it to be obtained. You take someone's word at face value because you say what you mean. But it's all based upon your station; where poor whites or whites with undesirable tasks or jobs would oftentimes be compared to that of the same level of slaves, showing that certain

---

[31] Thorp pg. 27-28
[32] Gorn pg. 33

tasks have certain standing in the culture.[33] It's where a slave can't spout off to the overseer or to the common white man without the risk of beating, so too did the southern yeoman farmer fear insulting the landed gentry.

This created a material culture that essentially created the symbol of masculinity, fortitude, steadfastness, and resilience. It's easy to see how this symbol of romanticized heroism reached its amazing crescendo with Bowie's death at the Alamo. It then became so important in southern frontier culture that it became almost akin to Samurai and their Katanas. It's easy to see how the southern Identity would grab ahold of that so easily to set themselves apart from the rest of American Culture. To pride themselves as more impressive, superior, with pride in all that they do, since they're not hiding behind the walls of an established city, they're going out into the wild and taming it.[34] It can also be argued that there is a stronger correlation and similarity of the southern Idea of the Bowie knife, due to the possibility that James Black used processes and techniques of metal refinement, heat treating, tempering, and edge finishing, that could be on par with Japanese sword makers. This potential similarity was also proposed by the author Raymond W. Thorp in his book *Bowie Knife* and if correct, this would mean that Black was capable of creating a weapon that is on par with the insane carnage caused by a Katana.[35]

Evidence can be found of this cling to the bowie knife and what it represented, and that no matter how bland the incident and lackluster it might've seemed, news reports always covered knife fights that occurred involving them.[36] This wasn't just isolated to the lower classes where the brazen knife fight was the solution for every infraction, but it became such an issue that not only were the upper class reported to have used them in duels, or in their education from aforementioned schools, but there are moments

---

[33] Gorn pg. 34
[34] Gorn pg. 34
[35] Thorp pg. 144-148
[36] Thorp pg. 47

where politicians openly attacked one another with Bowie knives while in session.[37]

Essentially, with the middle classes (which is the best way to describe them,) there develops their own little law of honor. This developed due to the lack of government, and more self-governing, or the law of the land, and settling disputes on your own. It developed this system that individuals had honor through their deeds and activities, so it was important to be the best at what you do, the best marksman, hunter, fisher, etc… and to be Masculine because it was akin to being powerful.[38] This standard of what made someone masculine, due to their daily struggle of living, created a sense of pride for one's self and created a system of honor that ultimately shaped everything. If someone insulted you, it mattered less if it was true or not, if it had enough merit to damage the image of yourself you've worked on, your place in the community could be taken into question.[39] It would affect you as a person and how you live and are seen for the rest of your life. The ideology of defending your place is what spurned the need to duel to defend your honor. There is a dynamic in the cultural system that tells them honor at all costs, if looked at through this lens while looking at the time right before the civil war, you see plantation owners being told that the economic system of slaver they built is morally wrong and that they must cease and desist immediately. This would financially destroy the south and everything they'd labored to procure.

In order to protect their interests, the landed gentry appealed to the simpler ideology of honor of the lower cast. They painted this picture to them claiming that their hard-earned way of life was going to be taken from them; the government was going to free all the slaves and because of this they would lose everything. This very much served as a catalyst to the idea of death before dishonor, and great glory for the South, and what better to hold this symbol than that of the Bowie Knife. You can see it early on in

---

[37] Thorp pg. 1-4
[38] Gorn pg. 35-36
[39] Gorn pg. 40

soldier's daguerreotypes which were sent home to their loved ones to remember them by while away; the southern soldier in full uniform, with garb, weapons, and shoved in their belts, right in the forefront for the world to see, was a Bowie Knife.[40][41] They were very eager and willing to romanticize this idea of leaving with their Bowie Knives which not only represented home to them, but with which they'd earned and defended their home, and had been wielded by a hero in the name of nation. They got so swept up in this thinking that it was evident in the letters that they wrote home; One such letter written by William Pender to his wife Fanny on May 16th 1861 read "I shall fight as if they were entering your dwelling, ready to give the deadly blow to my dear wife and child."[42] This delusion they had not only changed them in a way that they were unprepared for the horrific possibilities of war, such as their bodies not being buried and left to decompose in a field, or being indiscriminately blown up by a shell, but in other ways the romanticism of this cast system also carried over into their army.[43] Here it is evident that there was a real need for discipline in their army to suppress any perceived slights or honor squabbling between fellow soldiers. They very simply could not afford to lose men to duels over meaningless arguments and perceived insults; they needed a solid unit all working towards the same goal with the same enemy. This same time, the concept of what was considered hard work versus slave work, also had to go out the proverbial window in order to operate properly as an army.

Confederate officers had to instill the discipline of their men, and rework their mind to be willing to do the work that they deemed beneath them.[44] Sentiments very quickly changed once they started experiencing the war first hand and realized that this symbol of the frontier they were fighting for and system of economic based slavery wasn't being used the way it was supposed

---

[40] Berry pg. 172

[41] Fig 3-4 6-9

[42] Berry pg. 172, William to Fanny Pender, May 18, 1861

[43] Berry pg. 177

[44] Berry pg. 177

to at all.[45] This Bowie Knife that was supposed to be the shining light of an individual began to weigh on them. It began to take the fight out of them, as their mood noticeably shifted here because of that.[46]

The romanticizing of the sandbar fight that set the stage for Jim Bowie, to his legendary acts with a legendary knife, cutting down three men and reinforcing the prideful ideologies of southern masculinity. Combining that epic romanticism with the material culture of James Black being attributed to by making so many knives, here we see this culmination of a society that was struggling so immensely to rationally explain and maintain a feeble imaginative dream that broke well before it ended. This can all be summed up in one interesting and metaphorical way; Just as James Black forgot how he made the famous Bowie blade so too has history forgotten the importance for this symbol.

---

[45] Berry pg. 173-175
[46] Berry pg. 174

Fig.1 a basic Bowie knife.

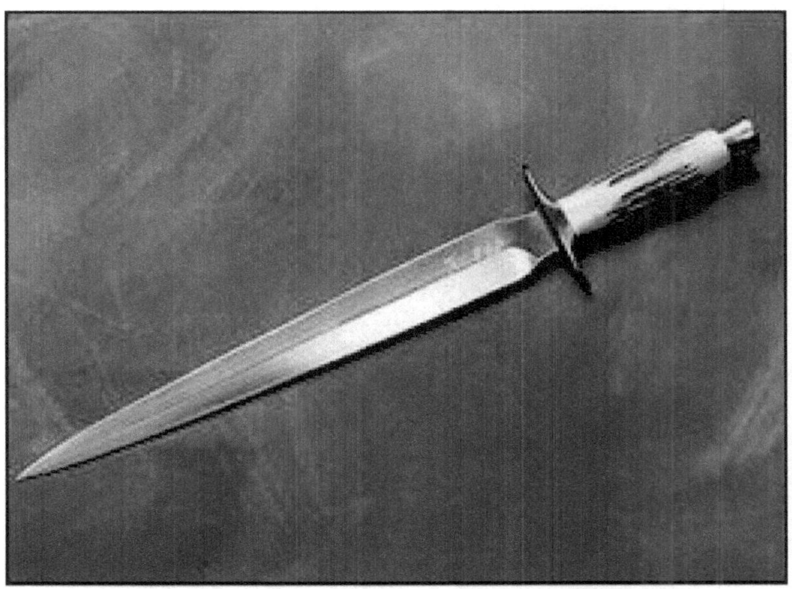

Fig. 2 reproduction of Arkansas Toothpick

Fig.3) Unidentified soldier in Confederate cavalry uniform with D-guard Bowie knife, revolver, canteen, and sign reading Jeff Davis and the South.

Fig.4) Sergeant A.M. Chandler of the 44th Mississippi Infantry Regiment, Co. F., and Silas Chandler, family slave, with Bowie knives, revolvers, pepper-box, shotgun, and canteen.

Fig. 5 James Black seated on right.

Fig.6) Lieutenant Hiram L. Hendley of Co. A, 9th Tennessee Cavalry Battalion with double barrel shotgun and Bowie knife.

Fig.7) Private David C. Colbert of Company C, 46th Virginia Infantry Regiment, with secession badge, canteen, pistol, and Bowie knife

Fig.8) Private David C. Colbert of Company C, 46th Virginia Infantry Regiment, with secession badge, canteen, pistol, and Bowie knife.

Fig. 9) Corporal John Agee Booker of Co. D, 21st Virginia Infantry Regiment, in uniform with Bowie knife, flintlock pistol, and tin drum canteen with his name on it

Photos Cited.

Fig.1 https://truewestmagazine.com/bowie-knife-fighting-blades-of-the-frontier/?fbclid=IwAR0bNCvSJj0qs2cs3E4XBphEM5N3rNQZM4L6myfrS4QyImGvHKIscjPoo2Y crafter unknown, circa 1830.

Fig.2 http://www.historicarkansas.org/collections/knife-arkansas-toothpick
made by Jimmy Lile, 1970.

Fig.3 http://www.loc.gov/pictures/item/2012650009/

Fig.4 http://loc.gov/pictures/resource/ppss.00834/

Fig. 5 https://truewestmagazine.com/bowie-knife-fighting-blades-of-the-frontier/?fbclid=IwAR0bNCvSJj0qs2cs3E4XBphEM5N3rNQZM4L6myfrS4QyImGvHKIscjPoo2Y

Fig. 6
http://www.loc.gov/pictures/resource/ppmsca.33334/?co=lilj

Fig. 7
http://www.loc.gov/pictures/resource/ppmsca.32064/?co=lilj

Fig.8
http://www.loc.gov/pictures/resource/ppmsca.32458/?co=lilj

Fig.9
http://www.loc.gov/pictures/resource/ppmsca.37289/?co=lilj

Works Cited.

• "Jim Bowie's Vidalia Sandbar Fight, Account in Niles | Lot #51011." Heritage Auctions. Accessed September 17, 2018. https://historical.ha.com/itm/miscellaneous/newspaper/jim-bowie-s-vidalia-sandbar-fight-account-in-niles-weekly-register-november-17-1827/a/6190-51011.s.

• HRISOULAS, JIM. *COMPLETE BLADESMITH: Forging Your Way to Perfection*. S.l.: NEPHILIM PRESS, 2017.

• Martin, Ann Smart, and J. Ritchie Garrison. *American Material Culture: The Shape of the Field*. Winterthur, DE: Henry Francis Du Pont Winterthur Museum, 1997.

• Thorp, Raymond W. *Bowie Knife*. Williamstown, NJ: Phillips Publications, 1997.

• Luskey, Brian, and Jason Phillips. "Muster: Inspecting Material Cultures of the Civil War." *Civil War History* 63, no. 2 (2017): 103-12. doi:10.1353/cwh.2017.0019.

• Gorn, Elliott J. ""Gouge and Bite, Pull Hair and Scratch": The Social Significance of Fighting in the Southern Backcountry." *The American Historical Review* 90, no. 1 (1985): 18. doi:10.2307/1860747.

• Berry, Stephen William. *All That Makes a Man Love and Ambition in the Civil War South*. New York: Oxford University Press, 2005.

Check out more cartoons like this….
www.leftycartoons.com

BUSINESS LOANS
AVAILABLE
APPROVAL RATE: 94.4%
CALL or TEXT
214-681-8400

A MIXED BAG *Of* FACT and FICTION

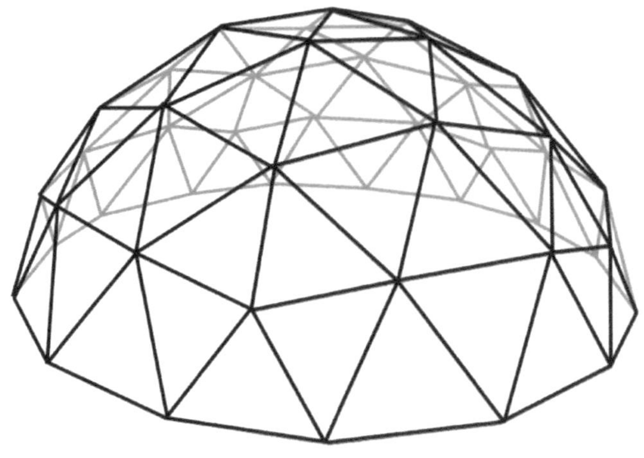

The Real National Emergency

America Needs to Build a Dome

By Bob Jensen

What is a real National Emergency? When do we put the United States on full alert? National disasters and War are usually the two top forms of national emergencies. In fact, they are the most legitimate forms of national emergencies. But there is something that's been happening in America that may be a true National Emergency and never gets talked about. Mainstream media has glossed over what is really happening and I feel like it's time to let the public know. It's not a crisis at our borders. It's not an economic crisis. It's not even a health care crisis. America has been invaded by aliens. No, not those kinds of aliens; the ones that have been here since 1947. This is the real National Emergency and our government hasn't done enough to stop the threat.

Aliens have been walking among us, we don't even realize it. Are they coming here illegally or are they invading America? We talked about building walls at our border to stop foreign Invaders, but what about the skies...do we have a plan to stop foreign invaders from the sky? With the creation of a new United States Space Force, it only stands to reason that we are preparing to deal with this threat. My investigation took me to a newly created Department of Homeland Security. It is called Extraterrestrial Section. And while it sounds like something from a science fiction book, it is quite real and a shining example of how our government is taking the threat of an alien invasion seriously. I spoke with the head of that department and for security reasons I cannot divulge his name so we will just call him Director X. He told me that when the department was created, their first task was to come up with a plan to protect the United States. The Plan called for a different kind of wall. While, Congress and the president are wrangling over funds to build a wall on the southern border of the United States to stop illegal immigration from Mexico, the Extraterrestrial Department of Homeland Security was coming up with a plan to build a different kind of wall and present it to the president of the United States. He stated, "this is the real National Emergency and we must act fast."

For security reasons, not many details were released about their plan. Please understand that I am not privy to classified information... There's only so much they could tell me. At the wall that they speak of is a dome. It is a dome that would cover the United States and protect it not only on all ground borders, but aerial borders as well. This Department of Homeland Security recognizes that the immediate threat doesn't just come from people crossing a northern and southern borders, but invading through the sky as well. As Director X put it, "if building a wall really is a matter of National Security then it must be the right kind of wall." It is being called The Dome Project. I asked him if aliens invading from the skies are really a huge threat, then why aren't we talking about building a dome around the entire Earth. Direct X told me that is far as the current Administration is concerned, we are only concerned about Americans.... That is how far we Humanity really goes and this is part of the new initiative of the United States government.

The Dome project sounded interesting, but I had to ask, if we are creating a space force, then shouldn't they protect us from an alien invasion. Do we really need a dime if we have the right weapons to defend ourselves. But I was told that the dome project is merely the last resort in an alien invasion, plus it already helps secure our ground borders so it's a win-win situation. I have to admit that this sounds a little overkill since there hasn't been any legitimate evidence of aliens truly invading America from the skies and it seem like wasteful spending. Director X said, "it's never too much money to secure America from all threats even if they may not be real...yet."

The plan has been presented to the president and according to sources inside the White House, he is thrilled with the idea. He has been quoted as saying "it's the best wall we can have and another thing that would make America great is to have the first Dome border on planet Earth. When I inquired about the budget for the Dome, I was told that it didn't matter how much it would cost and at what expense to social programs that helped American citizens like Social Security or Medicare.... the wall is the biggest priority in America and no matter how much it cost we should have a dome. Even though, the cost of such a program would be more than our national debt of 22 trillion. It seems for now that the president and homeland security are dedicated to seeing it built even if it's not a feasible which has been pointed out by leading engineering experts. One engineer pointed out that it would be more feasible to build an invisible force field instead of a dome, but the current rate of our scientific Endeavors in America, we are hundreds of years away from something like that being real. But that has never stopped our government from wasting money on stupid programs that we're never going to work anyway.

I think we should at least get the Star Wars program built, after nearly three decades before we move on to new programs. That seems more feasible than building a Dome. One source from the white house pointed out, "the president wants a wall or a dome, he's going to get it even if he has to make up a National Emergency to get it done. So for now it seems that

America's wall will now be a dome that will protect all Americans on every border and the skies from an alien invasion. But it does beg the question, is this so called alien invasion, the real national emergency.

Bob Jensen
Reporter & Columnist
The Squeeze
The more true news network!

YOU WISH ME TO SHOP FOR YOU?
ebay
DOOMLASER
YES! DO MY BIDDING!

We are always looking for submissions. We are looking for Short Stories, Poetry, Editorials and Articles (Non Fiction) and Cartoons / Comic Strips.

Submit your work to www.starvingwriters.net

Email us your submissions at...

submission@starvingwriters.net

9 781932 996708